LUSINE'S BLESSING

Printed in Australia
First Printing: September 2022
Shawline Publishing Group Pty Ltd
www.shawlinepublishing.com.au

Paperback ISBN 978-1-9228-5008-9
eBook ISBN 978-1-9228-5009-6

A catalogue record for this work is available from the National Library of Australia

LUSINE'S BLESSING

Will Spokes

Do you believe in miracles?
Lusine: Armenian girls name meaning; Torch of light.

Acknowledgement

For Willow, my own little Magic Princess.
Thank you for sharing your dreams with me.
Lyn, my wife without whom I would be speechless.

The Beginning

The Ancient Silk Road wound its way across the top of the world, from the Mediterranean to Japan, with branches forming a network running southwards into India, China and the Korean Peninsula, providing an important route for traders from every country in the known world for centuries. Many little settlements sprang up along the way, providing food and shelter to the caravans traveling the route. Some of these settlements grew into substantial trading centres over the centuries.

One heavily laden caravan was now returning from a profitable journey into India, where they had traded for all manner of desirable items including delicately crafted gold, carved ivory, jade, silks, embroidery and rare sought-after spices and was now returning home by way of the city of Samarkand in the south of Uzbekistan.

Seen from a distance, the caravan was shrouded in raised dust and heat haze, almost indistinguishable from the terrain it traveled through. Thickly coated in the dust of the deserts they had crossed; men and beasts were looking forward to resting in Samark and before resuming their journey homeward.

The weary caravan was far from safety and very wary, unable to relax their vigilance for a moment. The leader of the small caravan had chosen to travel along the bottom of a long and meandering valley, hoping to avoid notice and any further conflicts with marauding bandits. This was a very dangerous and turbulent time in the Greater Eurasia of the twelfth century. Khwarizmia, as this part of the East was known, had recently been dominated by the conquering Mongols who were cruel and pitiless invaders.

The observer would notice another dust cloud rising along the crest of the hills to the north of the caravan, parallel to their course. This would prove to be yet another bandit group scouting the caravan to plan an attack. The dust was noticed by the heavily armed caravan's escorts who immediately galloped into a protective position between the attackers and their charge. Meanwhile, the caravan gathered into a tight group behind their camels and horses, forming a defensive wall. The manoeuvre was performed swiftly and smoothly from long practice by the traders, who were also well armed and skilled in the art of warfare, more than able to defend themselves and their trade goods.

The skirmish was short and sharp. The escort was an elite mercenary group well paid for their bravery and knowledge of tactics and weapons. The observer would see these superb warrior horsemen drive through the attackers, splitting them into two groups, leaving some of the bandits lifeless on the ground. The escort then rounded on the now leaderless group to their left, driving them off inflicting further casualties. The bandit leader decided the risk was too high and with his force now divided, turned tail and disappeared over the ridge, having underestimated the strength of this relatively small caravan.

The caravan's journey had been very dangerous and more than once, they were attacked by bandits, who would take their goods and kill them all if they succeeded. For that reason, the caravan leader had wisely employed these mercenary Mongol horsemen to protect him and his investments, making sure to pay them well.

The leader of the caravan was a veteran of the Silk Road. His name was Kusan Avakian, a citizen of Yerevan, then the capital of Armenia. At its height, Armenia extended from the Black Sea to the Caspian Sea and from the Mediterranean Sea to Armenia. The country was sadly subjected to constant foreign invasions, finally losing its autonomy around 1400AD. The Armenian population was then at the mercy of the Ottoman and Persian conquerors for centuries. Kusan Avakian preceded all of that misery and was a seasoned trader who had become wealthy, with his eye for quality and knowledge of the markets. He was a strong and confident leader with persuasive negotiation skills and now was bringing home the results of his last rewarding expedition.

He would never allow these vultures to take his valuable cargo, the result of a long and arduous journey and much intense bartering. After many years of trading, this one last venture would ensure the future security of his family, waiting anxiously at home for his return and the guarantee of a comfortable retirement.

The city of Samarkand was one of the most important and well-developed communities on the ancient trade route. Its importance could be marked by the invaders that had taken it as a prize over the centuries, starting with Alexander the Great in 329BC and then, much later, the Mongols under Genghis Khan. Tamerlane was another very famous and powerful Mongol leader who ruled there.

Now in the mid-twelfth century, Samarkand was one of the greatest cities of Central Asia and a prosperous one due to its position on the Silk Road between China and the Mediterranean. The city was a centre for traditional ancient crafts of silk weaving, ceramics and embroidery, engraving on copper and the carving and painting of wood.

It was here Kusan Avakian would make one more trade that would dictate the fate of his descendants for many centuries to come.

Kusan's caravan arrived safely at last and he confidently negotiated care and shelter for his men, but ordered them to see that the animals are watered and fed before they take their own sustenance. Such is the importance placed on the welfare of the animals transporting Kusan's goods.

Kusan had a favourite inn where he had stayed on many occasions and was welcomed heartily by its proprietor. He was supplied with a room and a luxurious hot bath, after which he enjoyed a satisfying meal, then retired for a long and deep sleep in the first comfortable bed he had slept in for many months.

Kusan, by nature, was an enthusiastic gambler and an expert player of dice and tabula, an early form of backgammon, both popular games among travelers. Away from the sleeping area, he found a game of dice being played in a smoky room, noisy with the hubbub of a group of men speaking several languages all at once, yelling and gesturing to each other as they made their bets. Seated on rugs around a space where the dice were being thrown, were about a dozen very excited men.

Each one had a pile of coins before him and a large decorative hookah by his side from which they drew in great clouds of flavoured tobacco smoke. Kusan was familiar with this habit which he had first encountered during his Indian travels.

Kusan greeted the men and joined in the game, which continued for many hours. The men spoke of their travels and the price of the goods they traded. They discussed the bandits Kusan met and related their own experiences as they moved through the bad lands.

As usual, Kusan was successful at dice, being a cunning gambler. He scooped up his winnings and taking his leave, he decided to visit the city market.

He was known here by many traders and vendors and was greeted by them as they vied for his business, hoping he would take their wares. There was excitement and energy in the air after the desert that broken only by the creaking of harness and the complaining snuffles and snorts of his camels and horses. The men had marched alongside their animals stoically and quietly, saving their breath for things that mattered.

The marketplace by comparison, was deafening. Occupying a wide square are many traders and their wares are set out on stalls, tables or simply displayed on blankets spread on the ground. Livestock was contained in a number of pens on the edge of the market. Here there were many cattle, horses, camels, sheep and goats, all waiting to be auctioned. The noise and dust raised by the animals was deafening first and choking second.

There were hundreds of people jostling each other as they try to find the items they desire for their daily needs. Voices are calling in many languages, animals of all breeds are adding to the cacophony and the air is redolent with the smoke from cooking fires and animal smells. Exotic music could be heard from a band of touring musicians, playing for the dancers performing across the square. The air around the dancers was thick with kicked up dust and scented with the aroma of incense burning. Onlookers clapped their hands and called encouragement with that strange warbling cry from the back of their throats known as ululation.

Kusan's eye was taken by colourful silks and fabrics and the lush display of fruits and vegetables. His senses were assailed by the smell of spices and exotic food cooking over open fires.

The market place is noisy, bizarre and exciting and it brought an appreciative smile to Kusan's face. To him, it smelt like money.

He shrugged it all off and walked through the market and down a shadowy, narrow lane, out of the sun's burning rays where gold and silversmiths produced beautiful jewellery and where he had previously found some special items for each member of his family.

After bartering for some delicate gold and silver necklaces and intricate earrings for his wife and daughter, he was seeking a gift for his son that may help him increase his knowledge of the worldly matters of finance and trade.

As he passed a dark doorway, he was accosted by a man who appeared stressed and urgently insisted Kusan join him in his shop, as he believed a wealthy trader such as he would be interested in the curio he has had acquired. Kusan was offered a chair and when seated was attended by a woman who appears, offering refreshments presented on a large platter bearing dates, chilled water and fragrant herbal tea.

Almost without preamble, the nervous man produced what looked like a large book in the dim light of the ill lit room. On closer examination, Kusan found it was indeed a book, but a very curious one. It was quite old and heavy with its ornate cover of lambskin intricately illustrated with a strange design, the colours of which were almost bleached out, while its pages seemed to be papyrus and in relatively good condition.

But the very odd thing about it was the frame of ornate brass that enclosed the whole thing, making it impossible to examine the contents without first opening a formidable locking mechanism. The brass frame has decorative copper inlays and is quite beautiful, but marred by scratches gouged deeply into it around the lock.

The man's name is Tariq and he tells Kusan he had taken the item from the hands of a dying priest in a ruined temple after a Mongol raiding party had destroyed the village that surrounded it. Before he died, the priest or magus as he was known, told Tariq the book had great powers and could make the right man or woman into a sorcerer with the power to perform miracles. But in the wrong hands would destroy the holder by attracting bad karma to all his affairs. With his last breath, the priest begged Tariq to pass the sacred volume on to his fellow holy man in the next village.

Tariq was shaking and sweating profusely as he related his story.

Kusan's eyes had now grown accustomed to the dim light and could see the scratches were caused by someone attempting to force the protective brass bands open to gain access to its contents, obviously without success.

It was apparent Tariq had been overcome by greed and tried to gain the mystical powers the priest spoke of and had suffered the consequences of his dishonesty. In a series of misfortunes, he subsequently lost his wealth and his health and now he and his wife were in desperate straits. He fell to his knees and begged Kusan, who he was sure was an honourable man, to buy the item from him so he can be rid of its malice against him, resulting from his blasphemous assault on the sacred book and his betrayal of the holy man.

He told Kusan he could not bring himself to simply throw the intriguing object away, for fear of invoking further bad karma.

Kusan's curiosity was aroused and he impulsively agreed to give the man a handful of coins for the book and wrapping it in cloth he left without bothering to farewell the wretched man still on his knees, crying with gratitude as his sad wife comforted him.

Kusan had a friend at home who was a master of such things as padlocks and his plan was to take it home and present it to him to see if he could access its contents as it may contain the secrets of the universe or perhaps ancient cures for the diseases that ravaged mankind in those days. It required a key to access its contents and Kusan's expert should have little trouble manufacturing one. Unless he was very mistaken, this could be a very valuable acquisition.

Kusan meticulously recorded the details of the last few days, including the acquisition of the curious manuscript. The personal journal he kept would be read by his descendants centuries into the future. The journal recorded all his travels and details of his trades, profits and losses, battles with bandits and even weather conditions.

Time would prove Kusan's instincts correct as the manuscript and his journal were passed down the generations over centuries. The journal provided an insight into Kusan's life and business affairs; the sacred manuscript generating good and bad karma.

As it passed from generation to generation, it had a way of selecting its new enchanter (Magus) and anyone who tried to misuse its powers to increase their personal influence or wealth would be rejected in a most unfortunate way. Kusan's descendants inherited the volume and each generation learnt by experience, adapting to its influence, marvelling at its capacity to direct healing and goodwill. They also learnt from Kusan's example and maintained a family journal kept meticulously and added to over succeeding generations. When the sacred tome was in the right hands, the family remained healthy, crops thrived, animals bred strong healthy offspring and even the streams seemed to flow with cool, clear water.

Each succeeding generation, for the most part, conducted themselves prudently, keeping the volume a secret and using its powers sparingly.

The holy relic would only settle in the hands of an honest and virtuous person and was kept securely in a secret place. In times of trouble, the lock was opened and the manuscripts scanned for advice that never failed to provide a solution.

And so the centuries passed and the Avakian family thrived and prospered in their community until a great terror descended on the Armenian land, around the turn of the twentieth century when political turmoil and religious intolerance forced them to leave their much-loved home with as much of their wealth as possible they could carry. After a perilous journey across several oceans, they arrived in a new and sparsely populated country in the southern hemisphere.

The family name had changed as male heirs failed to be born and daughters married. The family that fled Armenia with the sacred relic were the Gasparyans, Aram, Marika and their children Ani and sons Barik and Petrak became the first of the family descendants of Kusan Avakian to arrive in Australia.

Aram Gasparyan and his wife Marika made Melbourne Australia their new home and joined the small Armenian community that had fled their homeland to seek sanctuary and stability for their families, like many other races fleeing tyranny and poverty.

Daughter Elen Gasparyan married Miklos Madaras and had a daughter of her own who she named Rose Alida. Rose married Tavit (David) Petrossian and retained the Madaras name. Rose would ultimately have a granddaughter named Lusine.

The sacred book that had travelled with the Gasparyans eventually came into the safe capable hands of Rose Alida (Petrossian) Madaras who would educate and mentor her granddaughter in order to equip her with the skills and wisdoms to become a strong community leader and the holder of the sacred book of the Magus and the enchantment it contained.

Lusine, Granddaughter of Rose.

Lusine Levy was to become an extraordinary human being, with an incredible inheritance waiting in her future. She was not quite there yet, but with the passing of her childhood years, she would discover a very singular and sacred bequest that would shape her whole life. But for now, she was another little girl dreaming of the princesses and fairies that populated the stories her father read to her each night.

Lusine was born into a warm, happy household in a lovely street in the leafy eastern suburbs of Melbourne. She was an only child, a lively dark-haired little girl who delighted everyone she met. Her smile showed perfect white teeth and her deep brown eyes would light up with special warmth when she met friend or stranger in a way that would melt the coldest heart.

Lusine loved music and dance and singing along with all the pop stars, while presenting her version of the dance moves she saw her favourites perform on the telly. Music was important to Lusine and her friends, taken everywhere with them on their iPods loaded with their favourite tunes.

Her father Gabriel (better known as Gab or Gabby) worked in the city and took the tram from the end of their street each morning after gently kissing Lusine on the top of her head, pecking her mother on the cheek and telling them both he loved them. He would be home again in the evening and the family would have dinner together and then go to their different chores.

Her mum tended to things like cooking and laundry with Lusine, helping her with both. She loved to stir the cake mixes and helped her mother load up the washing machine, doing as much as she could as a small child. As she grew, she took on more responsibility, making her own bed and even helping her father in the garden. Her father performed all the handyman chores and maintenance, like lawn mowing and carpentry. However, he insisted Lusine's schoolwork came before everything else, chores included.

With the passing of her early years, Lusine grew into a responsible and reliable young girl, so her mother had resumed her career as a lawyer, working mainly in the Children's Court, a role that often kept her late. At such times, Lusine and her father would prepare the evening meal, usually a stir-fry of one sort or another, which they found to be the easiest to prepare but also healthy and a tasty favourite. Lusine's mother was a member of the tiny Armenian population in Australia, so meals were often based on recipes from that culture. Her father Gab loved to cook the recipes from his Hungarian background, sometimes a delicious goulash. Her mother was always very grateful to come home to a hot meal after a long and often stressful day dealing with some of the most unfortunate cases in the big city.

Lusine felt safe and loved in her home and her bedroom upstairs was her very special space, filled with all the toys and books that she loved best. Her wardrobe was filled with beautiful clothes, including warm woolly jumpers that kept the cold out in winter and lovely, colourful summer frocks. As a pre-schooler, she was fascinated with the popular animated movies like Cinderella and Beauty and the Beast. Lusine had a clothing rack filled with the dresses of all the characters she loved so much; Cinderella and Snow-White filled her dreams. She still loved the movies and despite outgrowing the gowns, she did not outgrow the memories of the happy days they held and they would never be thrown away.

Lusine had some special close friends at school and she played with them at their homes or they would come to her house for a sleepover. They would eat popcorn and pizzas and all sorts of junk food while they watched movies on the flat-screen TV in Lusine's room. Lusine Levy was a very typical young girl of her time. The only thing that made her a little different perhaps was her maternal grandmother, Grandma Rose, who was from a long and interesting Armenian lineage with an extraordinary mystical quality.

Her grandmother wasn't odd in any obvious way; she looked like anybody's grandmother and walked proudly erect with her little black dog Ebony at her side. Grandma Rose was always smartly dressed in a slightly old-fashioned way, with a colourful brolly on her arm in the winter or a bright parasol in the summer.

Her long hair had become silver at some time and she wore it tied up in a chignon, often decorated with a fresh flower or colourful ribbon. In the summer, she preferred a wide brimmed sun hat that protected her fair skin.

But apart from that, there was nothing remarkable about her, except her eyes, which were a stunning bright blue behind rimless glasses perched on a slightly upturned nose. Her kindly face always wore a charming, friendly smile.

You would not really notice Grandma Rose coming towards you, but when she had passed, you would wish you had paid more attention to her, as a curious feeling swept over you, leaving a strange longing feeling for something missed.

Grandma Rose brought with her an infectious serenity wherever she went, leaving people with a feeling of wellbeing and the air redolent with her unique fragrances.

Lusine loved her Grandma Rose dearly and called on her often at her home on the next block. To get there, she would cross the tree-lined street, relishing the crunch of autumn leaves and the wonderful nutty smell they exuded when they were crushed under her feet. The deeper shade of the huge plane trees in the heat of summer provided a cooling respite from the sun's punishing rays.

The trees were beautiful, with their spotty trunks and funny little prickly seed pods. They made the walkways lumpy and bumpy as their roots grew grotesquely through the bitumen paving.

Lusine had a few scars on her knees, having tripped over them once or twice as a careless younger child, but no one would seriously think about removing the glorious trees that were the very essence of the neighbourhood.

There were possums in her street, the big fat brush-tail variety that crashed and banged on the roof as they squabbled noisily over the rights to Lusine's father's fruit trees in his back garden. Despite all of his attentions, pruning, feeding, watering and even placing netting over them in the early spring, the possums always seemed to find a way to beat him to his fruit. All of her father's dreams of bottling delicious apricots and peaches to be enjoyed later in the winter months disappeared into the fat furry bellies of the greedy possums.

Two houses along there was a delightful little laneway leading to a special space that would become very important in her life. The laneway ran between two houses that were set well back, giving the impression the lane was isolated away from suburbia. The lane was lined with self-sown flowering plants, including freesias in every colour under the sun, that burst forth in late winter and early spring. Their wonderful scent seemed to gather in an invisible cloud in the lane and was almost suffocating in its splendour.

Every transit of the lane brought a different delight, new blooms with their heady perfumes, dazzling shows of colour and sweet birdsong from a variety of fidgety tiny creatures, more imagined than seen, dancing among the foliage of the many acacias and other flowering shrubs.

Several wattles on each side hung over the narrow lane, their dense foliage meeting in places overhead to create a dreamlike tunnel. In the spring, when the wattle was in bloom, they showered the laneway with their spent blossoms, forming a dense golden carpet. It was only a very short walk before the lane opened up to a secret little magical park.

The park was situated in the middle of the block of private homes with no real access except through the lanes on either side or through private properties.

Local legend had it, the park had been the lush garden of a long-gone early settler's estate that had been broken up to form the estate that Lusine's house sat upon. Was Lusine the only person to feel the mysterious atmosphere of the park?

The property developers had perhaps experienced the surreal warmth that permeated the air and deciding the garden was too beautiful to destroy, left it as a feature of the residential area. The legend may have been true, but no one really knew.

It was a well-kept local secret the neighbours protected. Street parties were held there on special occasions and all the local children revelled in the safe playing environment it provided.

They played endless games of cricket or badminton with a net set up to one side in the shade.

The smaller children played hide and seek in among the park's profusion of plants and shrubs that provided many hiding places. Little girls loved the park, where they could lose themselves in daydreams of fairies and princesses.

If you asked who took care of the park, no one seemed to know. Everyone thought it was the local council workers, but no one could recall seeing them there with their noisy lawn mowers, trimmers and leaf blowers. And yet, mysteriously, it was always immaculately maintained.

Lusine would cross through the park on her way to Grandma Rose's home and exit on the other side by way of an identical laneway to the one through which she entered. It was a mystical little journey and her imagination would run away with daydreams of fairy queens and unicorns that she might meet here or the pixies and elves that sheltered behind the broad leaves of the hydrangeas.

In her imagination, the fishbone ferns provided climbing ladders for the tiny population who nested among the flowers, sharing the nectar with the tiny finches and honey eaters.

When she was younger, her mother would walk with her, but because she was such a sensible child and it was such a short and safe walk, she had later been allowed to go alone.

Sometimes though, as she walked alone, her imagination would conjure up the nasties in her bedtime stories such as evil queens, hungry wolves, cruel witches and spiteful hobgoblins that may be lurking in the shadows of the shady lanes, giving haste to her little feet. She would break out into the sunshine again and release the breath she had been holding as she scurried across the perilous ground.

As Lusine grew a little older and wiser, she knew there were no real dangers in the shady lanes. The only creatures she would encounter were the delicate little white-eye birds twittering and dancing from the twigs and branches as they searched for insects, tiny delicate skinks darting among the fallen leaves and the raucous cicadas that emerged from their underground burrows on the hot summer days, to sing at ear-splitting levels. Occasionally, the serenity of the park would be shattered by a squawking, screeching flock of rainbow lorikeets exploding into the park, the sun highlighting their bright bronze underwings and brilliant upper plumage.

They flashed past in a tight flock to feast on the nectar of the flowering gums bursting with colour to hang at all angles like jewels on a Christmas tree.

There was the ever-present grumpy chirping of the noisy miners that seemed to protest non-stop about anything and everything, especially intruders.

Sometimes rarely, she caught sight of the tiny spotted pardalotes dashing busily about or the brave and arrogant little willy wagtail, strutting across the grass followed by his harem of three or four wives. There were ravens here too, dressed in their jet-black silky plumage. Evil looking birds that wouldn't be out-of-place sitting on Satan's shoulder. They flew in from time to time looking for an opportunity to steal baby birds from their nests in the spring or pick up scraps dropped by careless children on their way home from school. In the very early spring, a mother wood duck could often be seen leading her little brood of ducklings waddling along behind her, towards the pond that was another feature of this lovely acreage, home to one or two tortoises and an assortment of loudly croaking frogs.

Every trip through the park to Grandma Rose's house was an adventure, sometimes scary (when Lusine was younger) but most times it was just fun and interesting.

Every now and then, a very curious atmosphere would come over the park. It could often happen in the late dusk as the sun slipped below the tree line as Lusine quickly made her way home. She was never allowed to make the journey after dark. Sometimes this phenomenon even occurred during bright sunshine.

It had happened several times before Lusine was really aware of it and then, when she did notice it, she sensed its coming and going quite frequently.

Lusine had once entered the park singing cheerfully along with her ever present iPod and while fiddling with the device, she removed her ear buds.

It was at that time she had first become aware there wasn't a single birdsong, not the smallest chirrup or tweet in the usually rowdy park. She had stood there stunned by the silence for several minutes when suddenly every creature in the park gave voice again at full, deafening volume.

After that first experience, she would stop and listen for that breath-taking silence. It was the first time she began to notice something else quite eerie.

She could swear she felt a disturbance in the air as though some large spirit had flowed silently and invisibly over her head, always coming from behind her, travelling towards the stand of lemon scented gums in the darkest corner of the park. There would be a pause of just a few seconds and then the park would erupt into its usual cacophony of bird calls. At first, Lusine thought she was having some sort of fainting spell as it left her feeling very odd, but then she rationalised it may have simply been a result of moving quickly between the different temperature zones of the laneways and the open parkland. There was nothing sinister about it, in fact, it left her feeling as though she had an invisible benevolent companion.

Lusine never mentioned these sensations to anyone, not even her grandmother.

Grandma Rose's House

But the best part of her little journey of several hundred metres was arriving at her grandmother's house. Grandma Rose lived in a rather large two-storey home known as Federation style that was built in 1890 on a large corner block. Although it was a very old home, it was beautifully maintained looking as though it were built only this year. It's style was known as a Queen Anne; an imposing rather fancy two-storey building with lots of interesting features on the outside. The roof was dressed with intricate clay tiles and ridge capping, ending with ugly gargoyles shaped like dragons or trolls on the ridges and the tower of the mansion.

The theme of grimacing figures was continued with a large and imposing door knocker, made in the shape of a fierce looking Medusa, her hair of live snakes gripping a heavy ring in her mouth mounted on a solid back plate. Grandma Rose said this ancient ugly design was to prevent evil entering the house, however, she preferred visitors to use the modern push button doorbell in the middle of the door frame.

It was indeed an imposing mansion-like property, with deep verandas that provided shelter from the summer sun or the rain storms of winter. Intricate stained-glass windows decorated the house and provided a wonderful kaleidoscope of colours that painted the interior's polished floors when the sun found them at the right angle. Inside were lots of decorative timber panelling and a huge ornate stairway that led to the upstairs area.

The stair posts had been shaped by the hand of a talented wood carver who had fashioned vines and flowers twisting and enveloping the core. Incredible dragons and strange winged creatures climbed among the vines with their tongues darting from their mouths like a warning.

Lusine had been intrigued by its design as a small child, often spending time tracing them with a chubby little finger, pretending to be startled by a carved lizard or dragon among the vines.

Grandma Rose was quite old now and found the stairs a challenge and spent most of her time on the ground floor where she had set up a bedroom in what had been one of three reception or sitting rooms, to avoid climbing the steep stairway. The room she chose had a large open fireplace that glowed with a bone warming log fire in the winter months and was delightfully cool in the heat of summer. Her bed was a large four poster style with an ornate canopy facing the fire and Lusine would share it with her grandmother when she stayed over.

It was wonderful snuggling down beneath her grandmother's big eiderdown bedspread, propped up by big fluffy pillows. She would lay there watching the reflection of the dancing flames and the warm colours of the burning logs, hearing the pops and crackles as they burned down to glowing coals.

Her dear grandmother would read her favourite stories until her eyelids grew heavy and before she knew it, she was waking to the sounds of Grandma Rose preparing breakfast in the kitchen and the chorus of birds creating a racket outside the bedroom window.

The most marvellous feature of the house was the huge kitchen where Lusine spent many happy hours with her grandmother, learning how to cook pancakes, biscuits and light-as-air sponge cakes. When she was little, Lusine would wash down her cake with the wonderful lemonade her grandmother made with the fruit from the trees in her backyard. Grandma Rose could make delicious baklava, lemon meringue pies and chocolate mud cakes. As she grew older, Lusine would join her grandmother with a hot cup of tea, taken with jam and cream on the fluffy scones they had just made together. Grandma Rose also schooled her in the traditional recipes of her Armenian heritage. Harissa-based on cracked wheat porridge and lamb, dolma minced meat and spice wrapped in vine or cabbage leaves.

She loved to sit in the large, overstuffed arm chair by the window where the afternoon sun would fall through onto her shoulders. With a tummy full of her grandmother's cakes and sandwiches, or sometimes on those cold stormy days, a delicious thick soup with those wonderful scones dripping with butter.

Grandma Rose varied the soups; chicken, vegetable and spicy soups, or thick magnificent lamb stews or peppers stuffed with mince and rice. With her tummy full, Lusine would curl up in her favourite chair and within seconds, she would be asleep, snoring contentedly.

Grandma Rose's wonderful house was like a cocoon of serenity and comfort. Lusine spent her happiest times there, learning to knit or crochet as her dearly loved grandmother patiently guided her impatient childish hands that before too long were producing beautiful delicate designs Lusine gave as cherished gifts to her extended family and school friends.

Lusine loved Grandma Rose's front garden. The entry gate was set back in a recess, sheltered by a gorgeous little construction of decorative timber fretwork and a little tile roof that imitated the roofline of the main house. The gate opened easily on well-oiled hinges and closed with a pleasing metallic clunk as the ornate cast-iron latch fell into place behind her.

Grandma Rose's Garden

The front garden was straight out of the TV program Better Homes and Gardens that Lusine sometimes watched, curled up on the couch beside her mother at home. Herbaceous borders consisting of foxgloves, poppies, ornamental thistles, grape hyacinths, daffodils, stocks, pansies, lupus spires and clematis all in riotous profusion. Gardenias and azaleas, rhododendrons, ferns, fuchsias and a brilliant cascading wisteria draped over one corner of the veranda, like a Spanish lady's shawl. In the permanent shade of the house, glorious hydrangeas grew. Their huge, bunched flowers of deep blue and pink were like small explosions. And all year round, the garden was heavily scented by one or several of the more dominant flowers that could instil serenity in a troubled soul. Lusine's favourite was the daphne that bloomed prolifically in late winter.

It was said that, 'music hath charms to soothe the savage breast.' Although she had never heard that quote, Lusine found the riotous profusion of colours and scents had much the same effect on her the moment she walked through the gate. All her childish cares would be washed away.

Grandma's backyard was more utilitarian, with a thriving herb garden close to the back door providing an abundance of parsley, thyme, tarragon, mint, rosemary and garlic and many other strange herbs Lusine could only guess at. Further into the yard were several beds that rotated crops of silver beet, onions, snow peas, lettuce, carrots, parsnips and radishes. Along the fence, rhubarb grew in abundance and joined the fruit from the apple tree growing above it in Grandma Rose's mouth-watering pies. The garden beds were set into the area of the yard where they would benefit from the most exposure to the sun all year round. The centre of the yard was given over to a beautiful soft and perpetually green lawn that never showed the wear and tear from Lusine's games with Ebony the jet-black little terrier, Grandma Rose's constant companion.

In one corner, a wonderful ancient oak tree planted by Lusine's great-grandfather provided a thick limb perfect for a garden swing on which she would try to defy gravity, to the horror of her grandmother, swinging high to the tipping point.

On the extensive verandas, Grandma Rose had some padded comfy sets of chairs with matching occasional tables arranged, along with a swing-chair. When the sun shone too hotly or the rain came down too long and too hard, they would seek shelter there and watch the garden fill with birds that gloried in the summer rains and bathed in the ornate bird bath splashing and squabbling with each other.

They admired the bossy noisy miners that took first preference over lesser species and who were beset by impatient bathers-in-waiting, such as the bold willy wagtails, the only other species brave enough to directly challenge the noisy miners.

The precious time Lusine spent at her grandmother's side taught her a great deal about every subject under the sun. Grandma Rose taught her the secrets of cooking and explained the mysteries of the herbs she grew and how they should be used to enhance a recipe. She taught her about growing those herbs and the importance of things like smelly fertilisers and correct watering and weeding. Lusine learnt when to plant seasonal crops and when to harvest them at the peak of freshness and flavour.

The gardens were quite vast and complicated and begged the question, how did her grandmother manage such an extensive plot as well as keep the house in such magnificent order? But Lusine never once queried her grandmother on the enormous amount of work it would take to maintain them. The ordered and disciplined way they presented which would exhaust a relatively fit man. But here was Grandma Rose in an immaculately tidy home in the midst of gardens as lovely as anything Lusine had seen on television. She simply took it for granted and her immature mind had not yet learned to query the things adults said and did. Her grandmother and her house and gardens were so special to her she thought little of where they had come from or where they were going and how all the enormous amount of chores received the attention they needed to keep things in line. Her father's garden by comparison, however, was a never-ending chore like painting the Sydney Harbour Bridge. No matter how hard he worked in it, his yard was always a bit of a shambles.

To Lusine's little girl's eyes, her grandmother's house was an enormous mystery that seemed to have a hundred rooms and a thousand places for her to explore and hide. It was a classic of its type and would grace the pages of any 'beautiful home' magazine. There was one area that contained a large ancient cabinet made from oak bearing evidence of its age with a scarred and battered exterior.

Lusine was never allowed into that strange space and was never told what the odd piece of furniture contained.

One cold winter's day, when she was a little older, Lusine's mother, Susanna Rose, sent her on a mission to her grandmother's house to borrow a special piece of crockery. Her mother was hosting a small group of work colleagues at the weekend and she was planning to serve one of her special Armenian recipes she hoped she could present in Grandma Rose's beautiful ornate tureen she had inherited from her mother, Lusine's great grandmother.

Susanna felt Lusine was responsible enough to take care of the precious item on the short journey from Grandma's to home and Grandma Rose was sufficiently confident of her to approve.

Grandma Rose had the tureen on the kitchen table in a protective cardboard box open at the top when Lusine arrived. Grandma Rose had it gleaming clean and looking very beautiful. This was a vintage Capodimonte (a famous Italian manufacturer) soup tureen with a matching platter and ladle, which made it a very rare and gorgeous piece.

The two ladies, Rose and Lusine, one older, one younger, chatted happily in Grandma Rose's warm kitchen, exchanging little bits of news and greetings from one to another. Knowing her mother would be anxious, Lusine picked up the box, finding it was a little heavier than she had expected, but not unmanageable.

She kissed her dear elder on the cheek and turned to leave. Grandma Rose walked her to the front door and held it open for her as she left with cheerful farewells.

Lusine walked along the street and turned into her enchanted park and would soon be home. She reached the end of the laneway and was turning into her street when she caught her toe in one of the large gnarly elm tree roots that grew up through the bitumen paving. She stumbled, letting out a cry of despair as she fell forward onto her knees, grazing them painfully and losing her hold on the box which flew through the air and emptied its contents onto the paving with disastrous results. The precious crockery clattered and shattered. The beautiful lid with its stylised rose-shaped handle broke into three pieces, followed by the body of the tureen and its platter both simply fragmenting.

Lusine was devastated and knelt on her injured knees over the ruins of her grandmother's prize piece of collectible antique crockery and burst into hot tears of shame and humiliation. She feared what her family would think of her now and what on earth she would tell her dear grandmother.

All she could do was pick up all the pieces and face the music. Wishing hard that she had been more careful knowing the paving was rough here, if only she could turn back time. She stretched out her hand to begin the sickening chore of picking up the shattered remains, her tears flowing freely now.

As her hand hovered over the pieces, the most extraordinary thing occurred. The pieces stirred, imperceptibly at first and then a little more rapidly. The movement became more animated and began to move very quickly, rattling together like a high-speed video re-assembling into their original form before her eyes until the beautiful item sat on the pavement without a blemish. The lovely lid sat separately from the ornate body on the rough pavement without the slightest chip or scratch.

Lusine was astonished. Was she dreaming? She looked around quickly to see if anyone had witnessed the impossible event and without further delay, she very carefully replaced the tureen back into its box with infinite care, almost expecting it to turn to dust in her hands. She wiped away her tears as she stood; the pain of her skinned knees confirming the reality of the bizarre event. She shook her head, still finding it hard to believe it had really happened. She nervously continued her journey, praying that there would be no further incidents.

But now she had a dilemma! Should she own up and tell her mother what had happened and what of her grandmother? What would she say? She decided she would see if her mother noticed anything and if not, she would stay quiet.

However, knowing how canny her grandmother was, she was sure she would never get away with the shameful secret. Perhaps her grandmother would also provide an explanation for the incredible event, which could only be the result of deception. But from where or from who? Had the fall shaken her up such that she hallucinated the dreadful loss of the tureen which instead had remained intact and secure in its box?

Three days later, when she dutifully returned the tureen, she was subjected to a stern and knowing look from her grandmother that told her somehow she was aware of her secret and Lusine was compelled to relate the mysterious story and beseech her grandmother for explanation. She was assured that understanding would come with time and now was not the time. She must simply remain patient.

Schooldays and Family Secrets

Lusine lived in that wonderful, carefree state as an adored child who had never experienced want or need and very little of that dark emotion — sadness. Except perhaps when she found her goldfish, Flash had died during the night and was floating on his side in his tank.

Life continued on in the same wonderful flow of seasons and events, days running into weeks and weeks into months and as time went by, Lusine's life subtly changed. She was in high school now; an exclusive private girl's grammar school fifteen minutes' walk away on the edge of her suburb. She was very lucky being able to walk to school with the alternative of catching a tram in wet weather from the end of her street. She left a little later than her father, but from the same sheltered tram stop.

Lusine loved school. As a senior in primary school, she had a circle of good friends she had grown up with through kindergarten and pre-school. Her teachers were kind and helpful whenever she was learning a new subject. School hours were filled with class time and sports. The girls played field hockey or soccer, netball and swimming. Lusine enjoyed playing soccer and as a very good swimmer, represented the school. She had learned to swim at an early age during the family holidays by the sea.

Theatre and dance were where she excelled and the school had a wonderful program she threw herself into energetically.

Like most year seven school students, Lusine had plenty of homework to do as well, especially mathematics and science subjects. Her days and weekends were full of activity in one thing or the other.

Everyone's life can at times be interrupted by something unexpected or accidental. Lusine was enjoying an almost idyllic life, as the weeks and months rolled out with never a pause. There were no untoward dramas in her life. Some friends had minor accidents that were a cause for much hype and there were one or two scandals concerning teachers' love affairs that rocked the student population and were the subject of delicious speculation in the playground for weeks. Petty feuds between different social groups on Twitter or Facebook that were more 'storm in a tea cup' exaggerated offence taking. All of this was pretty much normal adolescent stuff Lusine had no trouble navigating.

Her own group in school were classed as 'swats' that took their studies seriously and excelled at sports as well. It was a derisive term meant to inflict embarrassment on Lusine and her friends, but such was their strength of character, they shrugged off these pathetic tags by simply ignoring them. The school's leadership group, the school captain and the prefects were generally appointed from among these girls as they were seen to set a solid example to the rest of the student body.

Each year brought with it a more intensive school curriculum requiring more and more of Lusine's attention, but time slipped by pleasantly enough as she grew into a pretty young teenager. Lusine, however, was unlike any other and in her background was the accumulated wisdom of a family that could trace its history back to the twelfth century with a story as fantastic as any storybook snow queen and her handsome princes.

A wonderful thing happened when she had reached year ten. The children were considered responsible enough to begin studying chemistry and for Lusine it was a revelation. She took to it like she had been doing chemistry for years. For some unknown reason, when she opened her text books, she experienced something like instant recognition. She instantly understood the importance of the curious Periodic Table of the Elements. Oddly, all the elements on the chart seemed very familiar to her and as a result, she excelled.

She had an innate ability to understand the amalgamation of raw chemicals to achieve all sorts of amazing results that astonished her teacher.

Outside school, life did indeed cruise along blissfully for Lusine, who was about to get a very big shock. There was one very peculiar occurrence that at the time terrified Lusine and caused her to stop and reassess her grandmother and her generally serene character.

Lusine had received a very high mark in her chemistry studies and decided she would share her success with Grandma Rose by paying her an unscheduled visit late one weekday afternoon.

By the time she had completed her homework and chores, the evening was closing in rapidly and the light was fading.

She would have to hurry to avoid completing the journey in darkness.

As usual, she passed through her enchanted park, experiencing the same mystical reception that continued to delight her. When arriving at her grandmother's gate, all seemed well. The gorgeous gardens were in splendid order, as usual.

Darkness was descending rapidly now and she could see the grand house was dimly illuminated from within. The stained-glass windows reflected the light, which oddly seemed to be flickering like a flame.

Lusine was suddenly alarmed at the prospect of finding her grandmother's home in great peril from fire. She hurriedly mounted the steps to the veranda and cautiously approached the front door, her nose twitching for the smell of smoke.

Just as she raised her hand to the ornate door handle, she became aware of a powerful vibration running through the building like a low-level earth tremor accompanied by a low frequency moaning sound coming from within the house, filling the air around her. It was a weird, penetrating and disorienting sound, the power of which appeared to constrict her breathing.

Lusine then became aware of the sound of loud voices that could have been arguing or chanting in aggressive tones in some unintelligible language, gradually building in volume until she thought the whole world would hear them.

It sounded like at least three or four voices in some rough form of harmony.

She could not stand by any longer. Her dear grandmother must be in grave peril and she must do something to help her. Without any further hesitation, Lusine threw the door open and screamed for her grandmother. The reaction was staggering. A wall of sound struck her with a physical force that took the wind out of her, reminding her of when she fell out of her tree house at home and landed flat on her back and couldn't breathe.

Then came a silence so sudden and complete it created a bizarre vertigo effect. Lusine was stunned into immobility and stood rooted to the spot, her eyesight blurred and vague.

The house still continued to reverberate with the aftershock following the violent refrain. Lusine found herself shaking, her imagination running wild with fears for herself and her grandmother that something dreadful had occurred.

She called again, a little tremulously this time, her voice catching in her throat. Her eyesight cleared and several seconds passed before she realised her grandmother was standing in the reception space in front of her at the foot of the stairs. How did she arrive there, or had she been there all the time? Lusine could not be sure, but now Grandma Rose's face lit up with her beatific smile that pushed all doubt and fear aside as she walked forward and embraced her grandchild.

Lusine could not believe how calm Grandma Rose appeared as the old lady hooked her arm through Lusine's and guided her out to the light and warmth of the kitchen.

Lusine finally regained enough composure to put the obvious question to her mentor and received a gentle smile in return. Finally losing patience, she insisted she have an explanation.

Grandma Rose gave a little giggle and explained she had been listening to some opera on her ageing stereo system when the volume control jumped and the sound level went to the ear-splitting levels Lusine experienced. She had difficulty in shutting the unit down, eventually pulling the plug to do so.

Lusine suggested it was not like any opera she had heard before, but Grandma Rose told her it was Richard Wagner's The Ring and a particularly noisy version of The Ride of The Valkyries.

It was a reasonable explanation, but Lusine still felt there was something more to it than her grandmother was telling her. Grandma Rose appeared outwardly calm, but Lusine noticed her hand had a slight tremor as she poured them both tea and hoped she was not holding anything back. It would be inappropriate at that time to continue to press her on the subject and she decided to bide her time and hope her fears were groundless.

Later that evening, she related the experience in detail to her mother, who surprised Lusine by stating it was strange because her mother had always expressed a passionate dislike for the controversial opera, as it was reputed to be the favourite of the German dictator Adolph Hitler. Very strange!

Now, as a young teenager, a bit of reality was unavoidable.

Her parents required her to take on a set of chores around the home. Of course, she had to keep her room clean and tidy as she had always done, but her duties expanded to include helping her mother vacuum the large carpeted areas of the

Levy house and lending a hand with the laundry. Lusine was already an accomplished cook, so naturally she proved helpful in the kitchen as well. Her homework remained the number one priority before all else. She was now learning the importance of time management.

As all of this was going on, Lusine found she had less and less spare time to visit her Grandma Rose and sometimes she went two or three weeks without seeing her loving grandmother. She had been unable to resolve the mysterious episode that occurred when she called on her grandmother the last time.

It had left her feeling more than a little unsettled and she still hoped Grandma Rose might decide to reveal the truth behind it.

It became so long between visits that the park almost seemed unfamiliar except for one thing. That was the sensation of something unseen swooping silently over her as she entered her mystical haven and the almost deafening silence that came with it.

Her visits to her Grandma Rose, although infrequent by previous standards, were still a wonderful warm experience as she received huge Grandma Rose hugs of love. They would work in her herb garden, weather permitting, or cook up the wonderful cakes in the huge, wonderfully warm kitchen, as they had always done when it was cold and wet outside. As they worked, her grandmother would talk to her about her own childhood and growing up as a teenager in this very house.

Her father, Lusine's great grandfather, had been a successful merchant importing fabrics and spices into the country from all around the world. He was a descendant of a Middle Eastern family who were merchants trading along the ancient silk route through Asia. Lusine listened, amazed and fascinated by the stories her grandmother told her, thinking how exciting and exotic it must have been.

The passion in her voice as her grandmother related those legends so intoxicated Lusine that she could almost smell the spices and incense and hear the sounds of the pack animals, their harness creaking and groaning under the weight of the trade goods they were burdened with. On one occasion, Grandma Rose took some gorgeous fabrics from a heavily scented camphor wood box. She said they were the last gifts she received from her father and draped them around her delighted granddaughter's shoulders. The delicacy and vivid colours of the fabrics were astonishing and had an intoxicating effect on the young girl, swept up as she was in the romance of the stories.

Grandma Rose's talks kept on introducing her to a different set of her forebears, each with their own amazing story. The family tree stretched back hundreds of years into the ancient history of a fascinating and mysterious civilisation. She told of her ancestors who fought to survive in the dangerous and savage lands as they brought back their trade goods from the Orient. The trade route took them through scorching deserts and high mountain passes deep in freezing snow. The journey's hazardous conditions were made worse by the bandits waiting along the trade route to ambush them and steal their goods. They fought back bravely, inflicting many casualties on the bandits while the caravan marched on steadfastly and ever alert beside their heavily laden camels and pack horses.

Coming out of the mountains onto the plains below was no guarantee of safety, as the attacks were just as frequent and deadly in the desert. They would have to struggle to control the terrified animals as they tried to escape in panic from the clamour of battle, their handlers desperate to restrain them and fight off the assailants at the same time.

All of this was contained in the precious journal that had been kept by their ancestor Kusan Avakian as a record of his life and experiences.

Grandma Rose explained to Lusine that she was a Magus in the Armenian community and was considered a priestess.

She had been selected for that role by what she referred to as *The Blessing*.

When it came time, *The Blessing* would pass to Lusine and Grandma Rose would be there to help prepare her for that event somewhere in the future.

She told of the strange beliefs and customs conducted by the old ones to appease the God they prayed to and the religious icons she still protected in a safe and sacred place in her home. Despite Lusine's pleas, Grandma Rose would never reveal these items to her, nor would she display the journal and the sacred manuscript, as they were too delicate and far too precious to risk damaging them by exposure to the light. She told Lusine they were kept safe and in good condition, in a secure place within her home.

She warned Lusine in firm but gentle tones that she might find something disagreeable in that place, should she be bold enough to search for it. Lusine felt, quite reasonably, if Grandma Rose didn't want her to look at them, then she should not have told her about them.

Now, as a fairly normal teenager, she was instilled with a normal teenager's rebelliousness and impelling curiosity, but she respected her grandmother's wishes and would never do anything she felt would upset the old lady.

Grandma Rose told her, her induction might begin when she had grown into maturity. When Lusine asked when that might be, her grandmother said the final reckoning would be decided as it always had been by *The Blessing* itself. She would need to prove herself fit to receive that status. It could be when she had been presented at her debut or after her mother giving her approval. This would not happen automatically; it was an honour that had to be earned.

All of this caused Lusine's curiosity to peak and she pestered her mother for an answer that she could not, or chose not to, give.

Was her experience with the tureen some time ago due to these as yet unexplained and astonishing potencies?

Susanna Levy repeated Grandma Rose's words to her daughter every time she challenged her mother over the matter. All would be revealed after her debut when she would be considered to have reached maturity and not as a curious young teenager. She was told it would be best to forget about it for now and get on with her life.

Holidays and a New Friend

Holidays were a special time for Lusine. She thought she was the luckiest girl in the world as her father had many years before purchased a little cottage down the coast in a little fishing village called Port Isaac, named after a Cornish fishing village. Their little house wasn't exactly beachfront, which would have been far too expensive, but it was close enough to the beach that they could easily stroll down to the sand and surf carrying their water toys, sun brolly and ice box stuffed with sandwiches and cold drinks. Once across the main coastal road and on the foreshore proper, Lusine would be seen walking along with a colourful beach towel over her shoulder and a body board under her arm, her head down examining the sand for the tracks of the beautiful little lizards and the colourful Christmas beetles that populated the seagrasses along the side of the path.

The beach was a wide, clean crescent of golden sand that sat between two large outcrops of rock jutting into the sea, delineating 'her' beach.

It was hidden from the road by a stand of coastal scrub and the access track was hard to see from a passing car and had very few casual visitors. It had been her beach as long as she could remember. Very few people ever came here, possibly because of the hidden track or because the sea looked a little threatening, or maybe because of the dark, ominous rocks at either end. No matter, it was Lusine's beach and when strangers did arrive, she felt a flush of resentment.

But it was inevitable that as the city population grew and people searched for holiday destinations, she would have to share it with others sooner or later.

One brilliant sunny day, Lusine was busy decorating the huge sand castle she and her father had spent the morning building. She wore a large protective sunhat with a brim that bent down over her forehead protecting her face and despite her mother smothering her with sunblock, her nose was additionally painted white with zinc cream. Her swim costume was a modest but very pretty one-piece she found in her Christmas stocking, decorated with mermaids and dolphins.

The castle had all the desired features of a quality sand castle, large, elegant towers with castellation's and little slit windows, an imposing main gate made of drift wood with a drawbridge made of discarded ice cream sticks across a deep moat she was trying unsuccessfully to keep filled with bucket after bucket of seawater.

She had decorated the construction with several different coloured seaweeds and lots of shells that had washed up on the beach. It was without doubt the very best sand castle they had ever made and she stood back proudly, admiring it. Suddenly, a little dog with black patches over both its eyes, making it look like a tiny panda, burst out from the path onto the beach barking loudly with excitement at a flock of seagulls that had settled on the sand, sending them into panicked flight. The little dog's feet kicked up the sand behind it as it ran about excitedly, yapping at the gulls and running in and out of the waves, washing up the beach.

Lusine stood and watched, unable to take her eyes off the pesky animal. But then she started to smile and the smile turned into a giggle as she watched the frantic activity of the tireless little dog. Just then she heard a shout as a girl about her own age ran onto the beach, calling the dog back.

She had a surf board under her arm and her long blond hair was pulled back in a ponytail. She was suntanned and wore what was called a high cut wetsuit with a small backpack hanging off one shoulder.

She was a pretty girl with the skin peeling off her lightly freckled nose. She wore a baseball style cap pulled down to give that tortured nose some measure of protection. The dog spotted Lusine and took off like a four-legged bullet, his tongue lolling out, eyes lit with sheer joy.

Unfortunately, Lusine's gorgeously constructed castle lay in a direct line with the dog's headlong charge and he didn't bother to deviate. Before anyone could stop him, he had charged straight into it, bringing down the lovely castellated towers in a shower of sand and seaweed, then blundering through the main castle, totally destroying the lovely little moat and drawbridge in his eagerness to meet a new friend.

Lusine was horrified. The only dog she had ever had much contact with was Ebony, her grandmother's dog, which was exceptionally well behaved and would never create such mayhem. Lusine was no longer smiling. in fact she felt outraged and yelled at the girl to control her stupid dog.

The girl didn't seem to be too fussed by Lusine's annoyance and walked straight up and put out the hand that wasn't holding the surfboard and introduced herself as Shelley. She apologised on behalf of her dog she called Sharkbait. When Lusine questioned such an odd name, Shelley explained the dog went surfing with her and everyone knew sharks were supposed to be attracted to dogs in the water, don't they?

Lusine was instantly attracted to Shelley and forgot all about her sand castle, which suddenly seemed a little childish anyway. Shelley told her she had seen Lusine down here several times while she had been out riding the surf, generally in the early morning.

When it came time to leave, she would take a wave into the beach on the other side of the little right-hand headland to walk along the beach for a milkshake or a toasted cheese sandwich at the little café on the Esplanade. Sharkbait would already be there ahead of her, looking for a handout from Mrs Carter, who owned the café. This is why Lusine had never noticed Shelley before; she would have been just another anonymous figure way out there beyond the break. Shelley and Sharkbait were two very independent characters.

After this meeting, Port Isaac was never the same for Lusine. Her new friend Shelley was a local who lived just along the coast from Lusine's family holiday house and invited her home one day to meet her mother and have lunch together. Lusine was pleased with the invitation and after getting approval from her parents, the two girls walked off together along the beach passing by Mrs Carter's Café where little Sharkbait had already received a handout from the proprietor and was licking up some crumbs from the plate that had been put out for him. A short walk further on, with Sharkbait skipping along beside them as little dogs do, the two girls arrived at Shelley's home. Lusine came from a well-ordered tidy home and was unprepared for the mess that surrounded Shelley's place.

Her father was a professional cray fisherman who was always out at sea tending to his pots and bringing the valuable catch back for the market. When the weather was good, he would be away for several days at a time and when the weather was bad, he would be working on his boat, so he seldom had time to maintain his house. He was a good hard-working man who was born in the coastal town and was respected by his fellow fishermen and the general community. Shelley, as a local born girl, seemed to know everyone and everything about her home town and all the fishermen and she could tell the names of the fishing boats way out on the horizon even when they were little more than a tiny silhouette.

The front yard of Shelley's house was dominated by an old wooden clinker hulled fishing boat laying upside down on some old oil drums where the front lawn should be. A clinker hull was made of planks overlapping each other like a weatherboard house and needed to be carefully painted and sealed. Someone had begun a half-hearted job of sealing and painting the hull with an orange primer but apparently lost interest some time ago.

The old boat demonstrated its contempt for the neglected work by allowing one of its planks to spring open, rendering it unseaworthy. There was a rusty pile of old chain on the ground beside it and an ancient-looking anchor leaning against its side. The front veranda was a litter of cane crayfish pots stacked in careless profusion along its length. Coils of rope that looked well past their useful best, were tossed casually here and there. On the far side of the yard, in front of the main bedroom window, stood a scaffold arrangement with a block and tackle supporting a rusting diesel engine taken out of the old boat and left there to swing in the breeze. The whole yard was a tangle of weeds, with some brave little shrubs poking up here and there, looking very lost. Shelley explained her dad had beached the boat before she was born, intending to restore it but never quite got around to it.

They walked down the driveway and entered the house through the back door. The backyard was similar to the front yard, with lots of boating and fishing junk all over the place and a ramshackle shed that had more junk spewing out of it. An old dinghy with a set of oars leaned against the shed and it was hard to say whether the shed supported the boat or vice versa. The only clear space was the path from the laundry to the clothes line which was full of drying work clothes. Off to one side was a small garden planted with pumpkins and cabbages struggling to survive. The girls had to tread carefully as they entered through the laundry. Shelley's father had some huge sea boots and spray jackets taking up most of the floor space.

Lusine took it all in apprehensively, wondering if Shelley was embarrassed by the obvious neglect but she hardly seemed to notice and if she was embarrassed, she did a good job covering it up.

And it didn't stop there. About a dozen heavy fishing rods and reels were leaning into the corner of the wall and a tackle box sat on top of a pile of empty buckets stacked inside each other.

Sharkbait had a dog bed fighting for space just inside the door and his food bowl was upside down beside it. He sniffed the bowl, nudging it optimistically towards the girls a little as they came in, but met with bitter disappointment. Ah well, that's a dog's life. He would just have to wait for dinner time.

The inside of the house was as neat as a pin once they got past the laundry. Although the furniture was well used and a little worn, it was tidy and comfortable.

The kitchen reminded Lusine of her grandmother's kitchen and she instantly felt at home. The main feature was a large cooking range in an alcove with pots hanging from hooks above it. In the middle of the large room was a round wooden table with six chairs and a rack of condiments in the middle. Shelley's mum greeted them as they came in, with a big welcoming smile and introduced herself as Mrs McKittrick, but asked Lusine to call her Edie.

She placed a platter of sandwiches on the table and from a large refrigerator unit in the corner, fetched a carton of milk, setting it down with two sparkling, clean glasses.

Lusine looked around and thought there was no doubt it was the home of a fisherman. The walls were covered with pictures of old sailing ships and groups of men holding up big dead fish in different places and more boats; a powered one crashing through huge waves and a wrecked old ship on the rocks. There were beautiful sea shells on the sideboard and above the fireplace, some odd coral-encrusted brass bits dotted around the room that must have come from a shipwreck. On one shelf there were books on fish species of the southern seas alongside a big colourful dried starfish. There was an item Lusine recognised as a sextant, used by mariners for navigating the seas. It was all very nautical.

Needless to say, the two girls bonded as though they had known each other for years, providing an example of opposites attracting. Certainly the refined and ladylike Lusine and the boisterous surfer girl Shelley were an odd couple, but Lusine had never had a companion at the beach who was so much fun and with whom she had spent so much time.

As the holiday period went on, Lusine was paddling out with Shelley in the surf but with only a body board, she couldn't go as far as her new friend. Her parents were a little concerned about big surf even though she was a strong swimmer. Lusine only ventured out when conditions were moderate.

One day, when Shelley met Lusine at the beach, she said she had a surprise for her and pointed to a surfboard lying on the sand.

'It's yours to use whenever you want it,' she told Lusine, 'as it's my spare'. Shelley had begun calling her Ell for short, just like the super model, which embarrassed Lusine a little, but she secretly thought it was cool.

Shelley spent some time on the sand teaching 'Ell' how to stand on the board from the paddling position to the upright position. Lusine was quick to learn and before too long, she was surfing alongside Shelley. She was not as good as Shelley and would never be a great surfer, but she was good enough to have a great time.

The girls surfed until they were exhausted or the tide changed and the surf flattened out. Often they went back to Shelley's where her mother barbequed crayfish in the backyard or fresh fish baked in the oven in foil with lots of butter and lemon. They enjoyed lovely crusty fresh bread from Carters Bakery and Cake Shop and Lusine swore she had never enjoyed food more.

The holiday went by very quickly and before too long, it was time to pack up the Levy holiday house and head back to Melbourne. Her father would be starting work the very next week and they couldn't stay any longer and her mother was urgently required in the children's court, plus there was a lot to do at home and Lusine would have to start thinking about her school year.

For the girls, it was a sad parting, but Lusine promised she would be back in the first school holidays and on weekends in between.

Sad farewells and promises to keep in touch were entered into and finally a brief hug and Lusine was waving through the back window of her father's car as they motored out of their quiet little street and onto the highway back to the city.

A Coming of Age

Normal life would resume and the family of three attended to their duties in their own time and with cheerful discipline. Lusine resumed her visits to her Grandma Rose and found the little park just as enchanted and her grandmother's hugs just as warm and welcoming.

Lusine was now a little more forward in her thinking. Her education and limited life experience were beginning to develop her enquiring mind, which led her to question a lot of things she had previously taken for granted.

For instance, how did her grandmother manage to keep such a large household in such good order? There was scarcely a speck of dust or a streak on a window. The wood floors were always polished and shiny and the carpets vacuumed. And then there was the garden. That alone would, or should, be an almost full-time job for a healthy person. Yet she had never seen a gardener, handyman or housekeeper anywhere near the place.

Lusine pondered these questions and many more as she sat on her bed listening to some music downloads. She had questioned her parents almost relentlessly and they always replied the same way. Her Grandma Rose was a remarkable woman who had her ways.

What was it about the park she crossed through so often since early childhood? What was that curious feeling she experienced there that was like being enfolded in one of her grandmother's warm embraces? What was the explanation for the sudden silencing of the bird and insect life when she felt that invisible manifestation as it swept silently over her?

As she sat in her room, she became absolutely resolute in her quest to find the answers and there was only one person who could explain it all and Lusine was determined to take it up with her grandmother. She would remain respectful but firm when probing Grandma Rose for answers. For some time her grandmother had been schooling her subtly about her family history without being too detailed.

Was it in preparation for something greater? Now she would initiate the conversation again and see where it went. She was very apprehensive, nervous and excited about it, while being determined.

The next morning was Saturday and Lusine jumped out of bed, still determined to pursue the truth as today's mission. Her room was upstairs at the back of the house overlooking her backyard, with a bit of a view across the neighbours' sunlit rooftops. Down in the kitchen, her mother was rattling about making the pancakes Lusine loved every Saturday. Her father sat at the table reading his newspaper and drinking his coffee from the big mug she had decorated at school as a Father's Day present the previous year. It was a pretty ugly creation, but her father loved it and would never throw it away.

Lusine scoffed down a stack of pancakes, washed down with chocolate flavoured milk and was about to make a rapid departure when her mother pulled her up short, reminding her of her commitment to the household chores that were waiting. Reluctantly, she stopped and turned back. Her chores didn't take long and her excitement was giving her wings.

Lusine resumed her mission immediately and farewelling her parents, she banged out of the screen door and ran down her street to the laneway that led into the park.

As soon as she entered the laneway, she paused and stared in wonder at the beauty in this tiny sliver of her neighbourhood, rich in colour and heavy with the perfume of dozens of flowering plants, mostly self-sown.

She walked on through the lane, mentally rehearsing how she might diplomatically quiz her grandmother about the many mysteries that seemed to surround her and even emanate from her. As she entered the park, she paused, waiting for the familiar phenomenon that occurred each time she came. Three paces into the park and there it was; the distinct feeling of some invisible force passing overhead and immediately a pall of silence fell over the park. Oddly, it was a comforting sensation, rather than a threatening one. Lusine had subtly questioned several of her neighbourhood friends who also used the park, asking if they had ever noticed anything odd happening when they came into their special playground.

Most replied in a way that indicated the negative, along with a sideways glance at her to see if she was serious. One or two scratched their young heads and gave it thought before shaking those heads and moving away from her as if she might pass on a cold virus.

There it was. She was the only one for whom this, whatever it was, performed. Was it real, or was she hallucinating?

This was the incentive for asking the wise old lady for her opinion or advice on this and other conundrums, troubling Lusine's young enquiring mind.

Shortly she arrived at her grandmother's lovely old home, marvelling once again at the beautiful flower beds that bordered the path and framed the lush green lawns as she entered the ornate gateway. Grandma Rose's little dog Ebony greeted her at the gate exuberantly, bouncing up and down on his back legs, licking Lusine's extended fingers and running in tight circles around her feet as she walked up the path.

It appeared her grandmother was expecting her as she was sitting on her front veranda at the elegant little round table that was usually pushed into the corner whenever Lusine had visited previously. Instead, it was now more or less in the middle of the veranda providing a view of the whole front garden and was set with a brilliant white linen table cloth that fell to the floor on top of which sat a large tea pot, wearing a knitted tea cosy that kept the contents piping hot.

Also on the slightly crowded table was a tempting platter of cupcakes in a range of brightly coloured icings, some chocolate, some orange, some with a cherry or with little icing decorations.

Grandma Rose was dressed in one of her old-fashioned ankle-length frocks in a brightly decorated material of flowers and tiny birds that drew Lusine's immediate thoughts back to the birds in the park.

Grandma Rose's face lit up with that gorgeous, familiar smile that penetrated her granddaughter's heart like a soft, warm shaft of light each time it shone on her. Lusine experienced once again that wonderful feeling of absolute, unconditional love and comfort in her grandmother's presence.

She sat down on the other white cane chair that made up the setting, after giving her grandmother a huge hug and a kiss on both cheeks. Grandma Rose was very pleased to see her and said so in her soft, agreeable voice.

The two women, one old and one young, sat quietly, content with each other's company and sipped their hot peppermint tea sweetened with honey, saying not a word as the birds in the garden tried to outdo each other in birdsong. There were a number of cicadas and other insects lending their own particular tunes to the overall choral performance.

Lusine was just reaching for another delicious cupcake when her grandmother broke the silence between them.

She started by saying Lusine was now at an age where she should begin to learn more about her ancestors and her learning should begin today. There would be many questions that would arise as Grandma Rose spoke, so she implored Lusine to save them, as they would inevitably be answered as she went on.

Lusine was gobsmacked. Had her grandmother been reading her mind?

Grandma Rose began by laying out the family tree from the very beginning, back many centuries when the family ancestor was still plying the famous silk route across Asia. At this point she warned her granddaughter sitting before her, that what she was about to hear might sound unbelievable, or at the least, challenging, and it would be better if they moved indoors and made themselves comfortable in the guest sitting room at the front of the spacious house.

There, she would begin to learn and embrace her true inheritance. Lusine suddenly experienced a rush of several concurrent emotions: excitement, apprehension and strangely, a sense of déjà vu.

As they entered the room, Lusine noticed what appeared to be a large very old book or more correctly, an album of some sort on the coffee table placed between two over stuffed but comfy arm chairs, providing further evidence that her grandmother had been expecting her.

Could this be the fabled book Grandma Rose had referred to?

The room was a comfortable and airy space called an inglenook with an open fireplace that held bone warming blazes in the winter. Now in late spring, the sunlight seemed to reflect the colours of the glorious azalea and rhododendron blooms through the window, adding further colour to the bright warm light shining through the stained-glass windows into the room.

When they were comfortable, her grandmother began a long and very curious story.

Firstly, she explained that the Silk Route or Road was an ancient trade route stretching east to west from the Mediterranean Sea all the way to Japan. As a trade route, it was used by many different traders from many different nations such as Syria, Iran, Iraq, China, Malaya, India, Greece, Turkey and Armenia. Goods, culture and religious beliefs were brought back from China, Japan and all the Asian countries as they traded with each other over centuries.

This amazing mix of races and religions brought their stories and superstitions with them, passing the cold nights by recounting their legends and myths in the evenings around the fire at the caravanserai. (Resting places similar to today's truck stops.) Over steaming cups of tea brewed and served strong and sweet from huge samovars, the oral histories of the different tribes would unfold. As the hookah was smoked and passed around, some very strange beliefs were revealed and sometimes even stranger objects of worship or sorcery, looted from monasteries or the pilgrims travelling to the holy lands.

Richly decorated icons, weird amphora-like containers that the owners swore, held powerful remedies for every known ailment plaguing mankind in those days. Some would reveal for the purpose of trade rare and sacred amulets and manuscripts in strange languages that the owner would claim held all the secrets of the universe, the meaning of life and more. One need only translate them.

Lusine's ancient ancestor was an Armenian trader named Kusan Avakian, from the village of Yerevan, then the capital city of Armenia.

When he passed on, he left his journal to his descendants detailing his life and journeys that proved to be an invaluable reference to the times in which he lived and the journeys and adventures he experienced. It was his diary passed down through the centuries to all the following generations who preserved the amazing manuscript that now sat on the table between the two women.

His diary revealed how he was able to acquire the mythical book that resided somewhere in the care of Grandma Rose. He was a cunning trader who managed to trade a handful of coins for the richly decorated and leather-bound tome that was protected, or rather locked, behind brass bindings. It was secured with a solid lock the previous owner had no way of opening. Kusan's fellow trader had thought it held a curse that had ruined him. He had betrayed a priest to obtain it and he tried many times to open it for its secrets, unsuccessfully. The stubborn brass bindings bore the scars of his fruitless attempts, after which he had suffered a series of unfortunate events that saw him lose his wealth and his health. The poor man blamed his ill fortune on the book.

When he returned home to Yerevan, Kusan eventually succeeded in opening the book with the assistance of a friend who worked metal into many intricate and decorative designs he sold in the markets.

He was also an experienced thief who understood the mechanisms of locks.

Although he took a long time, he was successful in producing a key that opened the curious book. He was under threat not to open it without the presence of Kusan.

Family history shows the locksmith's curiosity got the better of him and like the legend of Pandora, he defied the order and maybe suffered as a result. When Kusan called to retrieve his property days later, he found his friend had been struck down by a mystery illness and passed away quite suddenly.

The book was waiting for him on a table outside the home of his friend, covered by a thick cloth. The widow of Kusan's friend believed the book held evil powers that had been the cause of her late husband's untimely death and now she refused to allow it or Kusan into her home. In those times these very superstitious people would always look for something to be responsible for changes in their fortune and the book being the most significant event in their lives at that time was, in her mind, the obvious cause of the bad karma entering her home.

Kusan had carried the mysterious volume to his home and placed it carefully in a secure place and despite having the key to access its secrets, it sat for a long time undisturbed. He was a superstitious man like most of his peers and was worried the book might carry some form of curse. On one of his journeys, he met a Magus who read his fortune, predicting a period of great power and influence.

Kusan spent many hours with the wizard and learned his future was tied to the book that resided in its place of safe keeping.

A magus was a type of sorcerer from a priestly caste in ancient Persia; a practitioner of magic whose skills encompassed astrology, alchemy and other forms of occult knowledge. He spoke to Kusan about the volume he had and told him rather than fear its contents, he should study and understand the wisdom contained in its mysterious writing. His opinion was, if the object did not welcome Kusan's attention, then he would be prevented from opening it and there was only one way to test that theory. The magus was intrigued by Kusan's description and offered to make the journey home with him to study the strange item.

Now armed with a key allowing access to the tome's contents, many months went by studying the book and the two men were in awe of the message the writings revealed. Written in a form of Sanskrit the magus was eventually able to translate, it was as though they were reading a handbook on another world, a parallel universe adding to the already impressive knowledge of the magus and lifting Kusan from his status as a well-travelled and worldly man, to the position of a high priest or scholar who, with mystical powers, became widely respected and whose advice was sought by his neighbours, the poor, the wealthy and the aristocratic alike.

This, said Grandma Rose with great solemnity, was the beginning of a long line of ancestors with a particular set of mysterious skills and knowledge they used with great wisdom, generally for the benefit of the wider community. This was called *The Blessing.*

Like many such things, there were very strict rules of governance growing out of experience that dictated its use. It transpired that the supernatural powers endowed by the book were enjoyed by only one member of each succeeding generation. No matter how many children were produced only one would receive *The Blessing* and that would not necessarily be the eldest or the male member of that generation. There was no right of entitlement for anyone, in fact another strict edict incumbent upon the holder, meant any demand on its powers to enrich or to be used to extend the life of the holder, would in some circumstances result in the holder having to pay a steep personal price.

Grandma Rose believed it exerted a positive influence over her and her environment from its place of safekeeping. It brought with it though, a great moral burden, an onerous responsibility capable of crushing a person of weak character.

Lusine may one day inherit the manuscript and could possibly become the next Magus, but only after a long and intense internship during which she would be tested constantly to assess her acceptance of *The Blessing* and *The Blessing's* acceptance of her as a worthy candidate.

At any time she might find herself rejected by the dynamism within the ancient tome. Grandma Rose was sure of her granddaughter's intelligence and strength of character, that had been demonstrated several times in her life so far.

Lusine listened intently as Grandma Rose preached to her the need to be consistent and not shirk the responsibilities that her 'apprenticeship' would demand of her.

Evil is always with us.

Grandma Rose had been speaking a long time and Lusine's head was spinning as her family's unique history was revealed to her. Grandma Rose took both of her hands in hers and told her the authority handed down over several centuries had come to Rose when she was a teenage girl, the same age Lusine was now. She had felt the onerous burden of the calling fall heavily on her at first, but with the guidance of an elder and the passage of time, she had learned how to give balance to the use of the mysterious powers she had inherited under the strict guidance of the lessons she read from the manuscript. Over time, she had enjoyed the capabilities it gave her, which enabled her to help the people she loved and provide certainty in their lives.

Her life became filled with the joy that comes from raising the hopes and dreams of ordinary people struggling with the adversities of life, to see them and their children bloom and prosper.

She was also sought out to give guidance to the local Armenian community, of whom there were many still respecting their ancestry and customs. Lusine was totally unaware of this, particularly her grandmother's current relationship to the Armenian community. Now that she was aware of it, she would share the responsibility after learning of the folklore and history of her ancestors.

Grandma Rose went on with further revelations. Her second cousin, Anahit, had proved to be a very strange person who was never seen nor spoken of in the family. Armenians like to name their baby girls Anahit, as they hope the girls will become as beautiful and gifted as the goddess Anahit was. Sadly, this was not to be, in this case and from an early age Grandma Rose's cousin became a disgrace to the family.

Grandma Rose believed she now lived in some remote area overseas and these days seldom came to visit her kin in Australia. She was the black sheep of the family Grandma Rose said and while she was anointed as the next in line to assume the responsibility, she had proved to be corrupted by *The Blessing's* potent mix of powers. Grandma Rose had to intervene. As an elder, she had dominance and had run her cousin and Lusine's great aunt Anahit off. Assuming responsibility for *The Blessing* as substitute Magus with the powers available to her, she stripped the black sheep of her potencies.

Realising Lusine was tired and overwhelmed, Grandma Rose decided to call it a day to resume again in the morning. The two women, grandmother and granddaughter, took a break and adjourned to the kitchen, where Grandma Rose made tea and sandwiches and placed a platter of her beautiful cupcakes out on the large oak table. The kitchen was, as always, a place of comfort and security, a familiar and warm sanctuary that carried many happy memories for Lusine.

But as they sat and restored their energy, Lusine was still speechless, her head filled with raging emotions and a hundred questions. Finally, it was just too much for her and she burst into tears. Grandma Rose was instantly at her shoulder, offering her a delicate embroidered handkerchief and put her arm around her distressed granddaughter, comforting and reassuring her that understanding would come and she would always be there as her mentor.

Lusine decided to stay with her grandmother overnight and called her mother, reassuring her everything was just fine.

Her mother had detected the emotion in her daughter's voice and was rightly concerned. She asked Lusine to put Grandma Rose on the phone. After speaking with Grandma Rose, Lusine's mother, Susanna, was satisfied that her daughter was rightly emotional, but safe in the caring hands of her grandmother.

Although it had been an emotion-filled day and Lusine's mind was whirling with all sorts of strange images, she was asleep as soon as her head hit the pillow. She slept soundly, waking at first light, feeling refreshed and strangely different, almost like an out of body feeling. She shook her head and swung her feet out of bed, ambling slowly to the big old bathroom where she found fresh towels and lovely scented soaps laid out for her. After washing up, she felt much better, but that odd sensation was still with her.

Lusine joined her grandmother in the garden, where they enjoyed a wonderful breakfast, with the early morning sunshine warming them pleasantly. As they ate in the lovely outdoor setting, the birdsong helped to soothe Lusine as she sat quietly and recalled her indoctrination to the family history the previous day. Ebony pranced around them excitedly, hoping for a scrap of toast or some other delicacy from the table.

Lusine held out a small crunchy piece of toast that was devoured in a millisecond and as Ebony licked his lips, she scratched him behind the ears distractedly. If what her grandmother had told her was true, then it seemed she was being prepared to be installed in an important and very responsible role.

So the thought that these powers her dear Grandma Rose spoke of were to be hers, was quite stunning. She would become the holder of the ancient truths and wisdoms as the magus-in-waiting.

Her eyes were focussed on a particularly beautiful cluster of freesias, overflowing the garden bed edging, their heady perfume already redolent on the morning air, when she experienced that strange feeling of some invisible being passing quietly overhead. She blinked, shook her head slightly and was back in the moment. She realised her grandmother was watching her with her usual beaming smile on her lovely face. Clearly, she was aware her granddaughter had just shared the experience of something surreal, but to her, familiar. Lusine caught her grandmother's eye and wordlessly, a great deal passed between them.

After they had cleared away their breakfast things, Grandma Rose announced there was a lot more to learn and if Lusine was up for it, they would continue.

They returned to the sitting room and took their places in the large armchairs and made themselves comfortable with another cup of herbal tea.

Grandma Rose gestured to the scruffy album-like book on the coffee table Lusine had noticed when they came into the room the day before and it had sent her wondering. This was not the sacred manuscript at the centre of their beliefs, nor was it Kusan's personal journal.

This was yet another journal that previous generations had compiled as a result of the example set by Kusan. This was a historical journal of the Madaras family back to the time of Kusan in the twelfth century; births, deaths and marriages all faithfully recorded, along with dates of significant events and movements. The whole text was handwritten on parchment that Grandma Rose handled with great reverence and care. Madaras was the name of her mother and grandmother's family. The journal was written in Cilician Armenian or Middle Armenian, as were many Armenian books between 1200AD and 1800AD. From the 1800s, English had become the favoured language. Grandma Rose had been schooled in the ancient language so Lusine would have to rely on her as interpreter if she wanted to access the earlier information. Grandma Rose encouraged her to become familiar with this strange language that would be so important to her understanding of her inheritance.

One very important date was the family's decision to immigrate to Australia. This occurred in 1915 when they fled ahead of the threat posed by the Ottoman government that had embarked upon a systematic annihilation of their Armenian population.

It was a very dangerous time for the Madaras family, who had some enemies in high places envious of their wealth and business acumen. These people could be relied on to betray them to the Ottomans, given an opportunity.

There were photographs of the old family residence in Yerevan, which looked quite grand and some old grainy photo portraits of the Madaras family that could have been taken inside their home, but more likely in the photographer's studio.

In the end, they had to simply walk away from their home with just a suitcase each as any attempt to sell their property would be seized on by their enemies as evidence of traitorous behaviour.

Aram Gasparyan and Marika had very early discerned the winds of change and had been able to transfer funds out of the country ahead of their departure and were carrying with them several ingots of pure gold and jewellery hidden in cunning containers within their trunks. If they were caught with this or they had been seen attempting to sell their property, the result would be internment and probable execution.

The supernatural abilities handed down over centuries were no protection against the racial hatred and institutionalised genocide of the Armenian population in Turkey and Armenia by the Ottoman Empire, that is still passionately denied by the Turkish authorities to this day.

In fact, their mystical abilities were another reason for the rapid departure of the Madaras family, as they were now being branded as a family of witches and warlocks by the very people they had helped over centuries with those self-same powers. Armenians were being exterminated, but not even *The Blessing* could help the Madaras family. Circumstances dictated they help themselves.

The portrait of the Madaras family was taken in a studio and showed a prosperous, happy group. Father sitting in an ornate chair as his wife stood beside him with their children arranged around them. There were three children and the journal revealed the sad truth that one child, a girl, was run down in the street by a bolting horse and cart. Their offspring suffered cruelly at this time with a series of fatal events. Another girl child was born healthy and strong during their subsequent sea journey and given the name Ani. She was a lovely girl whose exuberance helped heal the grief for the loss of their unfortunate child and their home.

The boy child Petrak, contracted Spanish influenza after arriving in Melbourne and quickly succumbed to the deadly virus, which took the lives of more than thirty million people around the world. Marika had inherited *The Blessing* by this time and was unable to influence the health of her son. That left just two children, Ani and Barik.

Lusine queried why those children died when their parents or siblings had such awesome supernormal invocations and charms available to them to prevent this.

Her grandmother explained very sternly that only God Almighty held the power of life and death. He had granted the Madaras family the miracle of laying on of hands to provide a cure but at an enormous price. If that power was used to extend the life or wealth of a family member, that price would be paid by present or future generations and therefore, had to be used with great circumspection. To even attempt to use their craft in such a manner was a grievous sin and would inevitably result in costly reckoning. This was an irreversible and sacred law that governed the lives and the actions of the hereditary Magus in the Madaras family. Grandma Rose's voice took on a grave tone that startled Lusine.

It carried with it an authority born of centuries of severe discipline attached to the responsibilities she carried. It was the voice of a high-ranking magistrate or priestess and was heavy with dread.

Grandma Rose then spoke sadly that she had watched her own dearly loved husband of many years David (Tavit), wither and die from a dreadful wasting disease and although she knew she could possibly invoke an incantation that would bring a cure or even relief from his dying agonies, she also knew the breaking of the vow would inevitably bring misery and pain to her descendants of whom Lusine was one.

David knew this and would not allow it, anyway. Could Lusine endure such pain for a loved one and remain disciplined to ignore her healing powers?

Grandma Rose softened her voice and went on to explain that *The Blessing* would bring joy and security to Lusine's life and she should not be afraid or disdainful of it.

Her grandmother would be beside her to guide her and protect her from temptation and evil and as they were just beginning their journey of knowledge, there was much to be learned yet and her lessons would give her understanding and with understanding would come strength, comfort and direction.

Arrival in the new land

Following an arduous journey across North Africa and Europe, the Madaras family finally reached England, where they could rest and breathe a sigh of relief. Aram, having arranged passage on a steam ship to Australia, called upon the Bank of England to establish his bona fides while waiting for the vessel that would take them to the great south land where they heard there were many lucrative opportunities in the burgeoning colony.

The family arrived in Melbourne and adapted quickly to their new home after sailing into Port Phillip Bay aboard a ship as unassisted migrants. There was very little border protection then and a baggage search was unheard of. So the family were able to bring much of their wealth with them, contained in their suitcases. Neither were there the banking regulations that monitor currency transfers in and out of countries. After transferring bank deposits to the Bank of England from Cairo, they were in a relatively safe and financially stable position. Aram, on his visit to the bank, had arranged for letters of credit to be forwarded to the Australian and New Zealand Banking Group in Melbourne.

But most importantly, they had managed to preserve and bring with them the religious icons and the Book of Kusan as it was referred to and the journal that Grandma Rose and Lusine were now studying.

The family departed from England as first-class passengers aboard the first available migrant ship for a journey that took 45 days to arrive in their new home on a warm bright summer's day, which they considered a good omen.

The family at that time consisted of Aram Gasparyan, Marika Gasparyan, Lusine's great-great-grandparents, their three surviving children, sons Barik and Petrak (who later succumbed to Spanish flu) and baby daughter Ani, born on the voyage. Aram quickly established himself as a trader, renting premises in Sandridge (South Melbourne). Later, as he prospered and his wealth increased, he purchased the building which remained in the family for over fifty years until the business moved to a more prestigious address in South Yarra.

As it happened, there were one or two mystics in Lusine's bloodlines, unknown to her until then. Her great-grand aunt Milena was one of those steeped in the ancient invocations and charms handed down generation to generation over centuries. Milena was able to cast spells and place a hex on her enemies, of which there were several. She was a white witch and the guardian of Kusan's Book, a wise and kind woman. Her daughter Anahit, heiress to the sacred lineage, sadly was the opposite of her mother, who when handed *The Blessing* on her mother's passing, created havoc and was totally irresponsible in managing the great temptations that came with it. This was when Grandma Rose, the next in line, took her in hand and stripped her of her power after a heated debate, supported by the rest of the family.

Anahit felt humiliated and betrayed by Grandma Rose's interference and in her shame, left the country to reside in Europe swearing vengeance.

It was Sunday evening when they wrapped up for the day and Lusine had a cracking headache, brought on by the immense amount of information and the incredible revelations she had experienced over the entire weekend. As they took a light meal, she pondered all the amazing information passed on to her from her grandmother who, until now, she had always considered a benign widowed lady living a quiet retirement in her beautiful home. But now the answers to some puzzles were being revealed, like how she managed such a grand home on her own. She guessed if you have amazing supernatural powers, would a little vacuuming present a problem?

She had one question before she left for her own home. One thing had fascinated her as a young child and still fascinated her now whenever she visited. It was the impressively ugly doorknocker, which seemed out of place in a beautiful home that held such sublime memories for her. Why was this ugly snarling head placed at her grandmother's front door?

Grandma Rose explained that it was the head of Medusa, a Greek mythical monster, a Gorgon generally described as a winged human female with living venomous snakes in the place of hair and anyone gazing upon her would turn to stone. It was called a preventive gesture, defending or protecting the household from disease or infection. Furthermore, anybody with evil intent could not pass. This and many other enigmas were unwinding for Lusine.

As she strolled back to her own home through the park, the invisible spirit paid her another visit but seemed to stay with her a little bit longer this time. She paused as she sensed it was circling around her and then swished silently away toward the far side of the park, as usual. Even though she was a bit late and would have to hurry if she were to get home in time for dinner, she paused to listen. She noticed the cicadas had been overtaken by the crickets as evening fell and the air above the park was filled with the silent flutterings of tiny insect bats eating their fill of the mosquitos and gnats that the lingering warmth of dusk had encouraged to dance before the rising moon. It was a magical time of day.

A New Beginning

The days began to roll out as usual, with school hours the dominating factor. She was constantly amazed by the stories of the supernatural world and sorcery revealed to her as her tutoring by Grandma Rose continued; but only after her homework and domestic responsibilities were addressed.

Lusine began to notice a new clarity in her schoolwork, her comprehension had increased and the mathematics problems she had previously wrestled with were suddenly no longer impenetrable, but appeared to unravel before her eyes. Her previously good term report became excellent, littered with A+s and wonderful comments by her tutors. Even her sporting skills sharpened up; her goal shooting in netball was amazing. Lusine was enjoying her life and it shone in her pretty face and her demeanour. No one would pass her in the street and not smile. Small children were attracted to her at parties and barbeques at her friends' homes. There were many more invitations than she could possibly attend as her schedule was now overwhelming, but she was always very gracious in her apologies for non-attendance.

The Levy family continued to holiday on the surf coast, where Lusine and Shelley McKittrick were joyfully reunited. Shelley would have Ell's (Lusine's) board waxed and ready to go. When they arrived, the girls would be off without waiting for the bags to be unloaded, whooping and screaming with excitement as they ran to the beach with their surfboards under their arms, little Sharkbait yapping at their heels with delight. Her parents didn't mind and went about opening the house for airing, laying out bedding and reducing the dust and cobwebs that had accumulated since their last visit.

The friendship between the two young girls grew stronger as time went by. Lusine stayed at Shelley's house now and again during school term holidays when her parents were too busy to go to their holiday house and Shelley stayed with Lusine once when she came to the city when her mother had business in Melbourne.

When they were together, they chatted like all teenage girls do, on fashion, music and boys. They shared each other's most secret dreams and plans and were closer than sisters, never having a cross word between them. When they were apart, they used all the social media that was driving the world. They texted, used FaceTime, Instagram and Twitter. All within the limits laid down by Lusine's parents, although her father struggled to keep up with some of the latest technologies. Her mother had attended training programs on all forms of social media, which was essential for her when dealing with young people in the Children's Court where she practised as a legal counsellor.

One night at home, the phone rang as they were having dinner. Lusine's mother put down her cutlery and rose to answer it. Gaby kept his head down, grumbling about inconsiderate people phoning at this time of night. Lusine was listening intently as her mother took the call.

She had an uneasy feeling about the interruption as generally calls coming like this were bad news. Susanna Levy handed the phone to Lusine. On this occasion, she was wrong. The caller was Shelley McKittrick, with the news she was coming to town with her mother for a couple of days and would be there tomorrow.

Lusine was excited to see her friend again until she asked why they were coming. Shelley's voice dropped and Lusine thought her heart would stop when she said she had an appointment at the famous Peter McCallum Cancer Centre. When Lusine asked if her mother was ill, Shelley replied with a quaver in her voice. No, it was for her. Her doctor had made the appointment after examining the lumps that came up almost overnight in her underarms.

She had been suffering night fevers, sweats and loss of weight. At first, they thought it was some form of anemia, as she was constantly tired. After further examination, her doctor suspected she was suffering a form of lymphoma and recommended she come to Melbourne for further testing.

After talking for a while and asking where Shelley and her mother were staying, they disconnected with a promise to speak again in the morning. Lusine's face was streaked with tears when she hung up and she could not stem the deep sobs that welled up in her chest in sympathy for her friend.

The Blessing

The next time the girls spoke, Susanna suggested Shelley and her mother join them for dinner. Her invitation was gladly accepted. The meal was a little awkward, with everyone making jolly and trying to avoid any further reference to Shelley's illness. When they had eaten, the girls were eager to be by themselves.

Susanna excused Lusine and Shelley from the table and went upstairs to Lusine's room, where they spent the rest of the evening chatting about the usual stuff that occupied their minds. Shelley told her friend not to worry about her, as she felt good and was confident her treatment would bring a positive result. Shelley and her mother departed after a relatively pleasant evening with the best wishes of the Levy family going with them.

Afterwards, Lusine sat down with her parents and they discussed the situation. Her father and mother who had become quite fond of the boisterous Shelley, suggested that as it must be a great inconvenience for the McKittricks to come to the city, that should they need to come again then they would be welcome to stay with them at their home as guests for however long they needed. There was the famous Ronald McDonald House that provided accommodation in these circumstances but the McKittricks were independent people and preferred to leave that to more needy cases. Shelley's dad had difficulty coming, as he was committed to his fishing and his pots.

Shelley's treatment went along the path of so many before her.

The awful diagnosis was delivered to adults and children, all people, rich and poor without favour. Anyone could be struck down by an illness such as Shelley's. There were many different variations of cancers. Some were deadly and swift and some were slow and lingering. They were not all fatal; advances in research gave many people hope of a cure and a return to their normal lives.

The one common factor shared by the survivors was their absolute will to win. They had an unshakable confidence in themselves and that was certainly Shelley McKittrick.

Supported by her friend, Shelley's immediate future would be tough, but she was full of confidence and possessed a cheerful resolve. Treatments for her condition were scary but applied in a careful, concerned and solicitous manner by the medical specialists. The extent of her cancer would be assessed first by a CT scan and bone marrow biopsy. Treatments might include chemotherapy, radiotherapy or a combination of both. Shelley would have to face a period in her young life far more frightening than a big wave or powerful rip. And just as she rode those waves to shore, Shelley would learn to deal with these waves and undercurrents.

Lusine was conflicted. Would she be able to use her powers to help heal her friend without suffering some chastening punishment? She went to her grandmother as soon as she could and beseeched her for advice and support. The response from Grandma Rose came in her usual gentle, but firm way as she reminded Lusine of the responsibilities that came with *The Blessing*.

She was also a devout Christian and warned only the Lord Jesus Christ had the power to cure the sick and raise the dead by the laying on of hands. For Lusine or any other holder of *The Blessing*, this would be a blasphemy that might bring down an awful wrath upon them.

She gently admonished Lusine for forgetting such an important decree so soon after her indoctrination.

Lusine was beyond disappointment. In fact, she was heartbroken for her friend and slumped down in her seat despondently.

Her grandmother's gentle hands fell upon her head and stroked her hair as she murmured quietly that she must have faith and be strong at all times for her friend and believe in Shelley's ability to fight for herself. As if to provide encouragement, Grandma's dog Ebony chose that moment to hop up onto Lusine's lap, employing his little pink tongue to gently stroke her chin while emitting a sympathetic whine.

Lusine slouched home in something of a daze, her mind fully occupied by all that was happening around her, such was her state of mind that she went through the park with her head down, blind to all its glories and its many and varied inhabitants both real and surreal.

When she arrived at her home, her mother was waiting with some sweet and sour news. Shelley was coming to the city again in a couple of days for further treatment. Her mother had rung and asked if they would still be welcome to stay over.

Of course they would be most welcome, replied Susanna and as soon as she hung up the phone immediately set about making the guest bedroom ready for their friends. Lusine was at once delighted and then sorrowful again for her friend and wished the circumstances were very much different.

The two days passed slowly until finally they heard the sound of a taxi's doors closing at the front of their house. Lusine didn't wait for the doorbell to ring and rushed outside to greet her friend and soon the two girls were jabbering away like a couple of magpies, both speaking at once.

Lusine's mother followed as fast as she could, but had no chance of keeping up. By the time she was out the front door, the girls were coming through it. They were pulled up short and directed to help Mrs McKittrick bring in the bags from the pavement where the cab driver had dumped them.

The next hour or so was such a happy cheerful reunion, it could be thought the girls had been separated for months instead of only a week or two. Lusine at her mother's direction had taken the guests bags up to their room and then she and Shelley had gone into teenage isolation in her room to listen to music and play video games. Pretty soon they were called down for dinner that was waiting for them on the dining table. The two ladies were laying out the cutlery and china while Mr Levy, who had been reading his paper in his big leather chair in the sitting room, folded it with exaggerated gusto and placed it on the seat of his chair as he joined them in the dining room rubbing his hands together in anticipation of the delicious spread before him.

Father took his place at the head of the table with mother to his right. The girls sat together on his left with Shelley's mother at the opposite end of the table to father. The next few minutes were punctuated by requests for this or that to be passed and then quiet descended, as they each attended to the business of enjoying the perfect roast lamb and baked vegetables on their plates. As they neared the end of their meals and the edge had been taken off their appetites, a little conversation erupted between the adults with questions after the health and wellbeing of Shelley's dad Danny and his fishing. It was peak season for him and he could not neglect his cray pots. The income was vital to provide for their immediate future. As they went on, the girls were excused and after putting their plates in the dishwasher, they ran off upstairs to resume their activities.

The next morning, a taxi arrived after breakfast to take Shelley and her mum into the Peter Mac, as everyone called it, for her treatment. Shelley had spoken about it to Lusine the night before and said she was nervous about it and hated the chemotherapy, as it always left her feeling weak and nauseous, but she assured her friend not to worry about it. She would be fine. That was like telling the sun not to shine, as Lusine lay awake all night worrying about her friend sleeping in the guest room across the hallway. She had to put it behind her now and smile cheerfully as Shelley drove away in the cab.

It was a school day for her and she had been falling behind a little by her exacting standards and needed now to give full concentration to her studies. She wanted to maintain the high standards that would be needed to gain admission to a science degree.

The temporarily separated family and their guests reassembled at the Levy home that evening. Shelley looking pale and drawn and unable to eat her evening meal. Lusine sat beside her and held her hand, trying to encourage her to smile, but it was hard work with little result. Shelley left the table with her mother and went upstairs to the bathroom, where Lusine could hear her retching and crying. Shortly, she heard the shower running and Shelley emerged later, looking a little better in her dressing gown and pyjamas. She went to Lusine, receiving a huge hug and then joined her mother in the guest room again to sleep.

The next morning was a Saturday and Lusine decided she would take Shelley to meet Grandma Rose. Shelley was still a little nauseous, but managed to drink a cup of hot peppermint tea with some jam and toast.

A Special Friend

The two friends walked arm in arm along the footpath to the laneway that would take them into the park. The elm trees were in full leaf and even though the morning air was quite warm, it was a very different atmosphere under the shade of their branches.

Shelley had never been here before and Lusine had never discussed it with her or told her about the peculiarities of the park. It would be difficult to explain to someone the surreal experiences she had had on her many trips to see Grandma Rose.

As they entered the laneway, she heard Shelley gasp and her arm muscles tense as she took in the amazing floral display Lusine had almost been taking for granted lately. Shelley stopped and stared at the array of colour and sniffed the air, appreciating the lovely perfumes floating heavily on the warm morning air.

Lusine was at first puzzled when Shelley paused and had to remind herself of just how stunning this patch of parkland beauty was and the effect it would have on anybody who had a soul. They walked slowly across the lush grass as Shelley tried to take in all the gorgeous blooms, pointing excitedly when she recognised flowers she hadn't seen in years. The seaside was not the place to grow a cottage garden containing the variety of plants here, so although they were familiar, they were very rare at home. Shelley laughed and said if they did plant flowers, her father would in all probability drop some old fishing gear on them, anyway. Not intentionally of course, but he came and went in darkness most often and would fail to see them.

The canopy of wattle had lost its golden glow at the end of spring, but the beautiful blue grey foliage still provided a wonderful shady cover from the sun when it grew hot in summer.

The park always had wonders for the senses, like the aroma of the lemon scented gums after rain, which was an intense joy.

Lusine was wondering if the invisible phantom would still make its presence felt while she had company and she didn't have long to wait for an answer. The entry to the park was sometimes an overload to the senses on an ordinary day, but today Shelley was treated to the full kaleidoscope of green hues sharply contrasted against the rich blooms of the flowering gums, azaleas and rhododendrons. The deafening chorus of birds and the competing variety of insect sounds chirruping, clicking and screeching made a continuous phantasmagoria of sound that would delight the most jaded park visitors.

The phantom stayed away, which was a disappointment to Lusine, as she was anxious to see if Shelley would detect the disturbance. After all this time, she had not shared the experience with anyone and was still uncertain if it was exclusive to her or her imagination. There was no ghostly intrusion on their journey and the industry of all the creatures in the park remained uninterrupted.

Shelley was very impressed with the secret park wandering about wide eyed, looking at the magnificent gum trees, the glorious blooms of the flowering shrubs and trees, closely examining the fine ferns and mosses that thrived in the deep shade of the larger flora.

Lusine told her how, when she was a little girl, she believed the ferns were inhabited by tiny fairies and elves and the colourful toadstools and mushrooms were created by them when they came out at night to dance in the moonlight and celebrate the stars.

Shelley kicked off her shoes and wriggled her toes in the lush green grass and spun about with her arms spread wide and her long blonde hair swirling as she arched her back and looked up at the pure white clouds; sheep grazing on the blue sky. She pointed to one cloud that had the shape of a dolphin broaching the surface as it pursued the bait fish it fed on. Shelley squealed with delight and ran around the outer edge of the grassed area. When she came back to Lusine, she was breathless and exhausted, but a huge smile brightened her face for the first time in a long time.

Lusine urged her on and before long they were entering through Grandma Rose's elaborate gate to the front garden with Shelley gobsmacked by the lovely old home and the beautiful flower beds and hanging baskets of petunias and the wonderful geometric patterns of the tessellated tiling on the steps and veranda.

Grandma Rose was in her garden cutting some gorgeous rose blooms, which she placed in a cane basket hanging from her left arm. To protect her from the sun's rays, she wore a very pretty sun bonnet and a light, silky-looking scarf about her neck. Her frock was another quaint ankle length cotton number decorated with images of fuchsias or some colourful flowers of one sort or another. Her hands were protected by white cotton gloves and in her right hand she held a pair of secateurs.

She looked like she was posing for one of those photos in an old gardening magazine. Grandma Rose greeted them with her usual warm smile and a hug for Lusine, who introduced her friend Shelley. Grandma Rose removed the glove from her right hand, which she offered to Shelley, who felt a warm tingling sensation when she grasped the old lady's hand in hers.

The two girls followed Grandma Rose into the house, where she removed her bonnet and led the way into the sunlit kitchen. First, she invited the girls to take a seat and excused herself while she took care of her flowers and washed her hands. In the twinkle of an eye, she produced a pot of tea and her familiar cupcakes and placed them on the big table, telling the girls to help themselves.

Lusine was feeling a little uncomfortable because she had come here under false pretences. She was praying that when her grandmother met Shelley, she would be immediately enamoured by her and agree to find a way to exercise her mystical capacities to ease Shelley's illness. At this point, Lusine was tight-lipped, fumbling for an opening on that particular topic.

The morning tea passed pleasantly enough, with Grandma Rose asking Shelley about her family and her life on the coast.

She enquired politely after Shelley's father and his trade as a professional fisherman. She pointed out that among Christ's disciples were several fisherman and Jesus would have a special place in his heart for her father, as Jesus called himself a fisherman for souls.

Lusine suddenly realised how intertwined her grandmother's beliefs were with each other. Christianity was a very big part of her life, whereas Lusine's parents gave scant regard to it. But that was the way of the western world at the moment; the younger, more prosperous and well-educated people were drifting away from the church, even though the country's whole social structure was based on the Judeo-Christian system of government and law. The church was seen by many to be losing its relevancy in today's society.

The Armenians from whom she was descended, were a strong Christian society with nearly ninety-five percent of the population declaring themselves followers of Jesus.

Later, Lusine would conduct her own research and find her ancestors worshipped in the Armenian Apostolic Church. This amazingly, was one of the oldest Christian churches in the world and the first to be adopted as a state religion.

Lusine watched her grandmother talking to Shelley and how she gave her friend her undivided attention, her piercing blue eyes locked on Shelley with their usual friendly twinkle. She was holding one of Shelley's hands now as they spoke and it was almost as if Lusine wasn't in the room.

Shelley responded to Grandma Rose in a soft voice, choosing her words carefully, aware of the great respect her friend Ell had for the old lady and not wishing to disgrace herself by saying something stupid.

The teapot was empty and the cupcakes all eaten when Grandma Rose appeared to reach a conclusion in her discussion with Shelley.

Lusine noticed her friend had a tear trickling down her cheek and when finally her grandmother released her hand, Shelley turned to Lusine with a sublime look of peace on her face and smiled widely. Grandma Rose stood and, as Shelley remained in her seat, put her arms about the young girl's head and hugged her into her bosom, muttering quiet words that only Shelley could hear. After which Shelley told Ell she was suddenly very tired and could they please return home to Lusine's house.

Well-mannered girl that she was, Lusine insisted on clearing the table first, then they thanked Grandma Rose for the tea and cakes and with a farewell hug for each of them, the old lady walked them to the door and wished them a pleasant walk home.

Lusine walked away with her friend bursting with curiosity to hear what her grandmother had said to Shelley, but Shelley wouldn't say, she just walked along quietly humming to herself as she hooked her arm through Lusine's elbow and dropped her head onto her dear friend's shoulder. They walked on like that until they entered the laneway, taking them back through the park to home.

Lusine wondered on the return if her personal spirit would make an appearance, as she had expected earlier in the day on their outward journey. She was not to be disappointed.

The two good friends continued on wordlessly and as they entered the laneway, Shelley's head came up and she seemed to come alight as they drew closer to the park entrance.

They had only taken two steps when the park went completely and shockingly silent. Lusine gripped her friend's hand and whispered urgently into her ear not to be frightened. Something was about to happen that she could not explain and Shelley would never forget.

Lusine need not have feared a non-appearance, as right on cue there it was, that stealthy visitor coming from behind them, swooping overhead and circling them soundlessly several times, but this time with a stunning effect.

Without warning, Shelley gave a loud groan and fell to the ground and began shaking and trembling as though she were fitting, with her eyes rolled back in her head. Lusine was horrified; she had never seen anything like it in her life and was paralysed with shock and fear. She screamed involuntarily and stood with her hand over her mouth, her mind racing. What was she to do? She had left her iPhone at home because Grandma Rose disliked them, so she was unable to call for an ambulance and if she screamed for help, no one would hear her. She took a step forward and then a step backward; she was now in tears turning around and around in panic. She couldn't run for her parents and leave Shelley alone. She felt helpless. Her heart was beating so fast and hard she could swear it would burst.

Lusine knelt down and did the only thing she could do by staying with Shelley and holding her hand, stroking her brow, talking softly and reassuringly to her, telling her she wouldn't leave her, when suddenly, Shelley stretched like she might do when she first awoke of a morning. Arms and legs stretched out to their limits, back arched and straining as she emitted a huge deep sigh, then she relaxed and lay still looking up at the clouds like she had never seen a cloud before, blinking and licking her lips as though she were parched.

Shelley looked up at Lusine, her eyes flicking back and forth, her mouth forming soundless words. Her dear friend looked into her eyes, frowning with concern at the distress Shelley had just experienced, and yet it didn't seem to have made any impression on her at all. She just lay there quietly on the soft green grass and after a few minutes she asked Ell what had happened? She said she had just had the most wonderful visions and why was she on the ground? How long had she been asleep?

Lusine helped her to her feet and brushed the grass and leaves from her friend's clothing, still looking deeply into her eyes, trying to discern her state of health.

She held Shelley firmly by the shoulders, imploring her to say if she was able to go on and was she alright?

Shelley shook her head like a swimmer coming up after a deep dive to blow out her breath and looked about the park, taking in all its wonders and laughed lightly and shook her head again, assuring Lusine she was fine. In fact, she hadn't felt this well for a couple of months.

Lusine was staggered; she couldn't believe what she had just witnessed. She had feared for her friend's life only moments before and now here she was bouncing about fully energised, her face flushed with the colour that had been missing over the weeks since she commenced her cancer treatment.

Shelley trotted along ahead of Lusine in a carefree manner, plucking a small bunch of deep purple grape hyacinth from the side of the exit laneway and holding it to her nose to breathe in its heady perfume. The girls arrived home in time for dinner, a traditional Armenian favourite of grilled dumplings made with minced lamb and served with yoghurt sprinkled with garlic. For sweets, Susanna Levy had prepared another family treat, a tray of golden baklava.

Lusine's mother took her aside quietly after the meal and questioned her about the noticeable difference in Shelley from when they left that morning. Lusine had no option but to tell her mother the full story of her grandmother, the park and its paranormal spirit and the frightening effect it had on Shelley and how she had bounced up afterwards, full of energy. Her mother was shocked but not surprised and crossly told Lusine she should have shared this experience with her earlier.

They would have to tell Shelley's mother, so she could inform their medical people, in case it was a manifestation of her ailment. They would be leaving early in the morning for a check-up after her chemo this week and then heading back to Port Isaac on the coast, where she would finally get back to school after losing a lot of time.

The morning sun rose bright and cheerful with a promise of a fine, warm, sunny day ahead. Shelley and her mother, Edie packed up their belongings and after thanking the Levys profusely for their hospitality, their car once again disappeared down the street with Shelley's hand waving from the passenger side window.

A Price is paid

The following weeks would provide some hard lessons for Lusine, as she struggled to deal with the enormous responsibilities that were being gifted to her. Her mother's aunt was the rightful heir to her grandmother's inheritance, but she had been side stepped because of what Grandma Rose said was wilful behaviour. Great Aunt Anahit had experimented with *The Blessing*, causing some very traumatic incidents that brought shame and harm to several important people. What those deeds were Lusine was never made privy to, except to say that in ancient times, they would have meant a severe punishment.

Was this a curse rather than a blessing? Grandma Rose spoke gently to her adored grandchild and comforted her by saying she had felt the same way when it came time for her to step up and shoulder this ancestral secret. It was not easy and it was unavoidable but as she said repeatedly, if handled skilfully, it would give her wonderfully uplifting moments, a great sense of achievement and the love and eternal gratitude of those whose lives she was able to enrich. Grandma Rose would be there for her, guiding her hand and deflecting any potential difficulties.

Lusine somehow found it difficult to see how it would happen and how she could live with those awful pressures.

Two weeks after going home to Port Isaac, Shelley had returned for further monitoring and testing and arranged to have dinner at the Levy's afterwards. When Shelley walked through the front door with her parents, she absolutely glowed with good health and energy, which shone out of her like a light.

The Levys were amazed at the transformation from the sickly child she had been in recent months to the picture of health that now stood before them. Only two weeks before, when she and Lusine had left to visit Grandma Rose, Lusine's parents were concerned for her and had urged their daughter to watch her carefully and be aware of her weakened condition that would lead to her tiring quickly.

Now Shelley stunned her friends with the news that her examination revealed no signs of her illness. None at all. It was as if she had never been stricken in the first place. The oncologists had never seen anything like it. Shelley was a real walking miracle and her mother standing behind her, broke into tears of joy and began hugging everyone in the room, once, then twice and was starting on a third round of hugs when her daughter brought her to a stop, causing the room to fill with laughter. Danny McKittrick stood there awkwardly; hands thrust deep into his pockets with a smile that threatened to split his face open, clearly relieved for his daughter.

Lusine was dancing with happiness as she hugged her friend, the two of them jabbering at each other at a million miles an hour but incredibly, understanding every word the other had said. The parents were doing their own version of a jabbering contest as a massive wave of relief swept over them all. Susanna Levy brought everyone back to some semblance of order as she called them into the dining room for the happiest meal they had enjoyed for a long time, the house echoing with their laughter and the rattle of plates and cutlery as they eagerly devoured another wonderful meal together.

Gab was pumping Danny for sea stories and the fisherman was keen to oblige, coming up with some fanciful and very funny salty tales. Edie had to remind him once or twice there were young ladies present, which brought forward further laughter.

The girls were allowed to go into the city by themselves, as Shelley had never done this before. All her previous visits were confined to the area around the Peter Mac and she was 'busting' to see all the sights. Lusine led the way to the CBD where they had coffee in the Walk Arcade, then attacked the big department stores and fashion houses. Then they crossed the river to Southbank and took the lift up the towering Rialto Building to enjoy the views across the southern suburbs and all the way up to the Dandenong Ranges and across Port Phillip Bay.

They had a wonderful lunch in a café on Southbank while watching all the joggers and cyclists weaving perilously between the wall-to-wall pedestrians.

They took a tram ride along Spencer Street past Southern Cross Station and made their way down Dudley Street to the Docklands Precinct, where they walked around the huge indoor football stadium. After having a quick look at the marina, Shelley said she was not impressed with the big fancy boats there. Slurping a huge ice-cream each, they reluctantly made their way back to the Southern Cross Station near Elizabeth Street to catch the 109 tram back home.

The girls had had a great day and after seeing the sights and grabbing some bargains, they stepped off the tram at the end of Lusine's street still feeling excited but becoming a little leg weary. They walked through the door with a big 'halloo' to be greeted by the parents who had taken advantage of the girls' absence to have a barbeque lunch and, judging by their flushed faces, had sipped a glass of wine or two in the sun without the benefit of sunblock or adequate shade. Or so they said.

The result was early nights for everyone and in the morning Shelley and her parents, with Danny driving and Edie waving farewell, left after enjoying a full breakfast taken on the patio overlooking the garden, where they were blessed with a warm spring sun. The girls said their farewells and were now looking forward to the next school holiday break, which would be their final year in their respective high schools. For Lusine, there was a science degree to be earned and a career in that discipline in some area yet to be decided. Shelley, on the other hand, had decided she would pursue Marine Biology, hoping to have a career in fisheries somewhere.

But before they started that serious stage of their lives, there was the Christmas holiday season that would see them surfing together again down the coast.

The girls in their separate realms put their heads down, working hard towards their final school results, hoping and praying for a score good enough to get them into the courses they wanted. Nothing else interfered with their studies, as they put everything into their work to give it their best. The really good news was Shelley's illness had shown no sign of recurring. In fact, due to her continued surfing agenda and consistent swimming, she had grown healthier and stronger than anyone would have expected only a few months before.

Lusine's mind, when she had a spare moment, would wander back to that day when she and Shelley had called on Grandma Rose and the scary 'fit' that had overcome Shelley and how she had improved in health from that day forward. It had happened as the unseen spirit circled closely overhead, something it had never done with Lusine. Shelley had fallen to the ground and fitted horribly. It was a very scary ordeal for Lusine. One she had never forgotten and as a result, had sought advice on how to help someone in that situation by undertaking a first aid course at her local St John Ambulance.

With her current workload and the excitement of Shelley's remission, Lusine was shocked to realise she hadn't called on Grandma Rose for a long time, in fact, not since she and Shelley had been there.

On the weekend, she rose from bed early, breakfasted and told her mother where she was going before setting off. Her mother said she hadn't spoken with Grandma Rose for a while herself and asked Lusine to pass on her best wishes and ask if there was anything she needed.

Lusine set off on her normal trip down her street and along her laneway to the park. As she entered the familiar area, she braced herself to receive the soundless spirit cruising over her head. She stood still and waited expectantly for the familiar rush and the stunning silence over the park, but something was different, completely at odds with her usual experience. There were a few bird calls and some crickets chirruping, but by previous standards, the park was practically silent. It had been a couple of minutes and she began to feel uneasy as she stood there waiting. Plenty of time for the spirit to come, but it had not appeared. She decided to move on. Maybe it was her long absence that was at fault. She would go on and see her dear Grandma Rose and talk to her about it.

Now her exams were over, she was on leave from school and would wait impatiently for her results to be published online in December. Hopefully, she would be celebrating with her parents and Shelley. And with lots of time on her hands, she would make up for lost time with her grandmother. She arrived at Grandma Rose's elaborate gate and walked into the garden.

She was surprised that her grandmother's little dog Ebony wasn't there as usual to meet her yapping excitedly, but the real shock was her grandmother's garden. The usual brilliant flower beds were wilted and brown, the lawn bore dead brown patches and the hanging baskets were in an awful state. Lusine ran up the path to the front door and rang the bell (she avoided the ugly door knocker) and waited for a response. She heard her grandmother's shallow voice calling her to come in and she nervously opened the door, which creaked noisily. It had never done that before.

She stepped inside, wondering as she did so, why she was feeling so nervous in a place that was always such a warm, comforting haven for her entire childhood. There was little Ebony walking slowly towards her as though he was unsure of who she was. She reached down and patted his head and his rump, noting his little tail wagging half-heartedly, but still wagging all the same.

The window shades had been drawn, rendering the house dark and even a little musty and airless. Escorted by Ebony, she found her grandmother in her bed on the ground floor in the former guest sitting room she had converted for the purpose. Lusine noticed the house was untidy and a quick glance into the kitchen revealed further mess. Lusine's heart jumped in her chest and she ran into her grandmother's room, where the old lady was tucked up under a large, colourful bedspread.

Grandma Rose's small bespectacled face poked up above the spread and was so pale and thin she looked almost translucent in the dim light of the room.

Lusine rushed to her bedside and threw herself on to her grandmother's bed, hugging her through the blankets, distressed at Grandma Rose's condition. The old lady asked Lusine not to be alarmed and when she withdrew her arms, her grandmother sat up wearily and asked for another pillow to be put behind her. She asked Lusine to calm down, assuring her she was just not feeling herself and to go into the kitchen and make some herbal tea. She would be out in a moment to talk to her.

In the kitchen, Lusine looked around in astonishment at the unaccustomed mess and began tidying up, putting some soiled plates in the sink and running hot water and suds on them. Grandma Rose never had need for a dishwasher. Meanwhile, the kettle she had placed on the stove began to whistle happily as it built up steam.

Lusine brought the tea pot over to the stove containing a favourite herbal blend of her grandmother's and poured in the hot water, releasing the aromatic steam which she breathed in, enjoying the wonderful freshness and delightful spiciness. A little shuffling noise behind her heralded Grandma Rose's arrival in the kitchen, followed by the scraping sound of a chair as she sat at the old oak table. Lusine turned and poured her a cup of the delightful tea, which Grandma Rose lifted unsteadily to her lips to breathe in the heady fumes gratefully. Lusine sat down and began sipping quietly until she dared to ask the question concerning her so deeply.

Very cautiously, she commented on the dying flowers in the garden. Was she having difficulty with watering? As diplomatically as possible, Lusine told Grandma Rose, she couldn't help noticing perhaps her grandmother could use a little assistance with her cleaning while she was feeling off colour. Grandma Rose said nothing. Lusine pressed on and told her of the negative experience in the park on the way to visit her.

It was like something sinister had entered the space where before, the park was a little patch of paradise on earth, where all the creatures rejoiced in their existence.

'All things have a time and a season,' said her grandmother rather mysteriously, 'and my season is passing. There is nothing to be alarmed about.'

Lusine was alarmed and softly demanded to know why her grandmother had not called her or her daughter Susanna to let them know she was unwell.

Grandma Rose carefully returned her cup to its saucer, took a deep breath and leaned back in her chair, looking grave. She told Lusine not to worry, what was happening she had been expecting. It was called *The Abdication*. It was, she said, *The Blessing* leaving her. Its powers slowly fading away as the brilliant colours of dawn do when the sun rises. The colours fade but the sun still rises to shine its warmth down on the earth from a blue sky. This condition would pass and like the sun, she would carry on and cope with what a normal life should deliver in the absence of her spiritual powers. Lusine's head was spinning. What was this she was hearing about 'abdication' and 'powers fading'? Was her grandmother telling her she was dying?

And why was *The Blessing* passing or 'fading away'? As her grandmother said. Suddenly, with an almost physical impact, an appalling thought popped into her head.

Was this somehow related to Shelley's extraordinary experience and her miraculous recovery from her life-threatening illness when they had last visited? Lusine needed to know.

Shelley had spent some private time talking quietly and earnestly with Grandma Rose during her visit. Neither one had included Lusine in their discussion, but it had a profound effect on Shelley. Later that evening on the way home, Shelley was overcome by the invisible presence collapsing to the ground to Lusine's horror. After an interval, she managed to rise shakily from the ground to begin an amazing physical rejuvenation.

Lusine looked on stunned and amazed by this apparent convulsion and rapid transformation of her friend from delicate to robust good health. She concluded that it may have been due to something unthinkable. This abdication may have resulted from her grandmother's selflessness.

But as Shelley's health improved, it seemed Grandma Rose's health declined. Was this the unthinkable result of *The Blessing* being used for the personal benefit of a family member? Shelley was not family, but her illness had affected Lusine very deeply and her recovery was certainly a personal miracle that changed the direction of Shelley's life and the same could be said for the Levy family as well.

Now shockingly, Lusine realised her much loved grandmother may have sacrificed her own health, depriving herself of her life force to save Lusine's friend Shelley. She recalled how she had begun her indoctrination with Grandma Rose into the acceptance of *The Blessing* and how she was warned about the improper use of the powers that came with the gift. It cannot be used for personal reasons without suffering a harsh consequence.

Had her grandmother taken that risk in extending her gift to help Shelley and was she now paying the price? Lusine was horrified and overcome with love and gratitude for the dear lady who would put herself at risk for Lusine's friend. Perhaps she had miscalculated and thought as Shelley was not a direct member of her family it wouldn't have the same outcome.

Lusine was sure Grandma Rose was a highly intelligent woman and the very last person to make a mistake like that. The only possible conclusion was she had acted deliberately, knowing she was breaching a very solemn vow. Without doubt, *The Blessing* was a very strict task master and excused no one.

Lusine held her grandmother's hands and looked into her eyes and found she did not need to speak any words as a powerful telepathic connection between the two women transmitted everything she was querying. Yes, her Grandma Rose had done what she did, not so much to save Shelley's life but to shelter her precious granddaughter from the grief of watching a childhood friend die from an incurable illness and inevitably falling to temptation to use her own powers to save her friend thus putting herself in grave danger.

Lusine had a huge burden to bear now as she was totally immersed in the teachings of *The Blessing* and would need to be fully aware of the responsibilities if she were to carry the ancient belief and practices forward for another generation.

The two women hugged each other as only two people with tremendous love and respect for each other can. Tears flowing freely, slowly they separated and Lusine set about helping Grandma Rose tidy the house and as the sun reached its zenith, shining warmly down upon them, she made a light lunch of sandwiches and more tea and as they had many times before, took it out into the garden. Ebony seemed to have had a fresh start, as he regained his usual vigour.

He bounced about with an energy level that put a lie to his earlier languor. The sun was as bright as ever and there were still many birds coming down to sip daintily at the bird bath and favour Lusine and Grandma Rose with a song.

They sat quietly in the comfortable, well-padded outdoor furniture, each one lost in their own thoughts when Lusine became aware of a slight tingling in her fingers. As she looked at her hands, turning them over curiously, the tingling spread slowly up her forearms to her shoulders and then she experienced a warm flush with the most amazing sense of rapture, causing her to shudder as though shaking off the cold. Her grandmother was watching her intently with those piercing ice-blue eyes that seemed to penetrate Lusine's very soul.

Quite soon the sensation passed and Lusine became aware of her Grandma Rose's knowing eyes upon her, aware of what had just transpired. Her all-knowing grandmother rose from her chair and embraced Lusine and stroked her troubled head with the assurance that what she had just experienced was *The Blessing* settling upon her. Ebony seemed to have noticed Lusine's reaction and jumped up into her lap, nuzzling his cold, wet, little nose into her chin.

From this moment on, she would be the Magus with all the strengths, knowledge and powers transferring to her in a manner somewhat like osmosis, as it infiltrated her every nerve and fibre. The wisdom accumulated over nine hundred years by her predecessors all the way back to Kusan Avakian, the medieval trader of the eleventh century who captured *The Blessing* in his incredible manuscript and held it safe for future generations. The Magus had traditionally been a male role, but as the centuries passed and suitable heirs had failed to materialise, the role fell to women who in Grandma's opinion had performed admirably.

The two talked for several hours, Grandma Rose telling her in her usual soft and passionate voice the things she might expect to experience. It was she said, not for the first time, that Lusine had been honoured with her selection by the spirit of *The Blessing* to have the necessary strength of character to be a suitable novice and her grandmother could not be prouder and more confident that she would be a wonderful wise and generous Magus. The inheritance and history of this exotic title was a direct connection to Lusine, all the way back to the birth of Christ. The three wise men that paid homage to the infant Jesus were believed to be the first of the Magi. This was a stunning revelation; one she would need time to digest and one that took her breath away.

Lusine suddenly felt a huge weariness descend upon her and with Grandma Rose's love and best wishes, she left for the walk home.

Looking around the slightly neglected garden, she shook her head and vowed to be more attentive to her grandmother and would recruit her parents to assist. The old lady appeared to be sickening with something and they would need to keep an eye on her. The abdication of her powers had laid her bare to illness.

On her way home, Lusine re-entered the park, her mind overloaded with everything that had happened on this incredible day which had passed in a flash. It was now getting on towards sundown and she realised her parents had been expecting her home for lunch.

In this dreamlike state, she was suddenly snapped back into the present as the park erupted in a massive explosion of sound from birds and insects that shook the air in a riot of song. Birds wheeled about her and the cicadas seemed to reach new heights with their ear-splitting cacophony.

There were swarms of insects providing an inviting target for the fluttering black bats that were putting on a flying display in the fading daylight as they gorged on the airborne bounty.

To her now wide-open eyes, the colours in the park stood out brighter and more intensely than she could remember; the contrasts were starker and the shadows more defined. The fern trees' fronds waved in apparent greeting on the gentle breeze cooling the park. The gorgeous pungency of the understory of flowering gardenias and daphne that still lingered after a long spring season were delightful and soothing. It was as though the park was trying hard to atone for its poor performance earlier in the day.

Lusine arrived home and went straight up to her room, closing the door behind her and threw herself onto her bed and was instantly, deeply asleep.

Her sleep was disturbed around dawn with strange vivid dreams of violent people, improbable creatures and voices calling from a long way off, sounding like they were coming down a tunnel. When she woke, she still felt exhausted and now confused by her vaguely remembered dreams. The sound of the voices was still echoing in her ears. The words were comforting and supportive in a way, although they were indecipherable. There was also a feeling she was being alerted to possible danger from some as yet unknown source.

It took some time for her to gather her thoughts and bring herself into the moment. A hot shower and her familiar morning routine helped, but she still felt as though she was emerging from a long and very detailed dream that started with her first otherworldly experience in the park and including her grandmother's revelations the previous day. She was at a loss to understand the processes she had just accepted as her inheritance.

Did she really have some sort of mysterious powers that would enable her to heal people or save them from difficult situations by influencing the events around them? It appeared an impossible thing, utterly unbelievable, but how else could she explain the weird and wonderful happenings that occurred or seemed to occur at her grandmother's home?

The immaculate gardens and impeccably kept household that one fit single person would struggle to maintain, but somehow her grandmother managed it.

She was determined to find out more when she returned to the old lady's house later that day.

Understanding and Reflection

Over the ensuing days and weeks, her grandmother schooled her gently and continuously in the wisdoms and lore of *The Blessing*. There was a lot to learn and so far Grandma Rose had not introduced her to Kusan's sacred book, which was the potent nucleus of their creed. She had delicately queried her about its presence and Grandma Rose gently diverted her queries, always maintaining control of the discussion. Lusine was convinced by what her grandmother didn't say, rather than what she did say, that the book existed and it would be only a matter of time and patience before it was brought before her and she would be permitted to use the sacred key.

Meanwhile, Lusine's learning was brought to a halt by the Christmas holiday break. Her hard-working parents were tired and jaded by the stresses of their occupations and were looking forward to their annual visit to Port Isaac and a long and lazy summer by the beach. So with the usual military precision, her parents, Susanna and Gabriel, packed all the necessary clothing and a large box of fresh green groceries and refrigerated goods.

Lusine had farewelled her grandmother, smothering her with hugs and kisses, promising to call her every day and before she knew it, she would be home again and they could resume Lusine's learning.

The first time Lusine's nose had picked up the wonderful smell of the sea, her heart lifted and a rush of childish excitement had flooded through her system. All her fears, doubts and concerns were immediately left far behind and she could barely constrain her impulse to leap from the car and run onto the beach and plunge into the beautiful crashing surf heard clearly from the car as it rolled down the slight hill and onto the esplanade heading into the village.

Arriving in Port Isaac, they picked up fresh bread and milk at Carter's Bakery and Cake Shop. Mr and Mrs Carter were delighted to see them again and considered them locals. Having exchanged greetings and barbeque invitations, they drove around the block to their holiday home. Gabriel jumped out of the car and circled around the exterior of the house, making sure everything was in order, while Lusine and her mum ferried all the items from the car into the house and set about making it all settled and homely. Food was first packed away or placed in the fridge, then beds were made and all that remained was to get the evening meal underway.

Lusine cheerfully volunteered to do that while her mother dusted and aired the bedrooms. Before too long, the house filled with delightful cooking smells and the table was set for four. Her mother knew it wouldn't be long before they had a visitor who would join them for dinner. They barely had time to set when Shelley rushed in, hugging everyone in sight, the girls squealing and shouting their news at each other before Susanna clapped her hands and issued orders to wash up and take a place at the table.

It was all a bit odd given the girls spent so much time on Instagram and Facetime that one would think they had exhausted all possible topics, but of course, there was always plenty to talk about. Ed Sheeran had toured and the girls had been part of the screaming mosh pit. Sia, the strange one with the odd wigs, was still cool in the girl's opinion.

New fashions and trends, favourite TV shows and fad foods. And then there was the surf. Shelley gave a complete run down on current surf conditions and predictions for the weeks ahead. She also quietly briefed Lusine on some of the surfing hunks in town for a sponsored event coming up. She was taken by a particular guy named Jake Turneau from further west around the coast. Everyone called him JT and he was ultra-cool.

The meal was long over and the girls' extended chat session had come to an end as Susanna suggested it had been a long day and they had the whole summer ahead of them. Shelley took the less than subtle hint and arranged for Lusine to meet her on the beach in the morning, where Lusine would show off her new radical board. The tide would be high in the early morning and the wind would be offshore, making for perfect surfing conditions.

Next morning Gabriel Levy rose early, almost as excited as the girls and went straight into the kitchen and put the kettle on. Apart from Susanna's soft, faint snoring in the bedroom, the house was strangely quiet. He went and ducked his head into Lusine's bedroom door and found the room empty and the surfboard, that should have been standing beside her bed, was missing. No Sherlock Holmes required here. The girls had hit the surf before first light and would be out the back of the break waiting for the tide and wind to deliver those glorious six foot glassy swells that are every surfer's dream.

That's where the sun found them, bursting above the eastern horizon, challenging the few clouds that hung low in the sky as if to suppress its' mighty rays. Instead, he painted them in splendid pinks and reds for a brief moment or two before lifting above them haughtily into his azure realm. None of this wonder was entirely lost on the girls sitting on their boards semi-submerged beneath them. Lusine was looking around her, once again thinking herself the luckiest person on the planet and staring down into the astonishingly clear water that darkened suddenly as a large shadow glided sinuously directly below her.

It took her a moment to comprehend what she had just seen.

Involuntarily, she issued a loud startled scream alerting Shelley, who looked at her stunned, shrugging her shoulders and arms up in the universally recognised gesture for, 'what the hell?'

Lusine began paddling furiously for shore, yelling at Shelley to get out of the water when the dark, sinister shape materialised beside her again. The shape was taking an uncomfortable interest in her and a shock of dread ran through her, generating a huge burst of adrenaline and the ancient flight instinct.

In a split second, the shape crossed beneath her board, coming to the surface on her right-hand side and exhaled a loud and very smelly fish scented breath that embraced Lusine in its full aromatic glory.

Instantly, she was laughing and screaming with delight as the big female dolphin rolled on her side, a beautiful expressive eye looking directly at Lusine. The characteristic smiling mouth opened and shut in a loud wet clapping sound as if the dolphin was greeting her and saying welcome.

By now Shelley had caught on and watched from her position so as not to startle the creature and ruin the spectacle Lusine was enjoying. She need not have worried because rather than move on, the lovely mammal wanted to stay and talk some more, or so it appeared. It circled and dived and rolled, performing some of the tricks of those poor trained animals in marine zoos around the world. After a brief display, it shot off swiftly out to sea, much to the disappointment of the now super excited girls who were laughing and squealing with delight. With all her experience on the sea, Shelley would be expected to be a bit blasé about just another dolphin, but this display was something she had never seen before and she was just as excited as Lusine.

Their excitement had begun to ebb slightly until happily the dolphin returned and instead of bursting from the sea, it approached her a little more slowly and it wasn't until it was almost beside Lusine again that she saw the reason.

The dolphin was a mother and she had brought her very young calf along, proudly showing it off like any young mother with a new baby. The mother nudged the baby towards Lusine, who was able to reach down and lay her hand on the baby's back, just behind its dorsal fin. She felt a strange sort of energy pass between them and at first, she wasn't sure which way it flowed, but it soon became apparent it was a discharge of energy from her recent endowment. The little creature appeared to shudder with pleasure and then it went into a rapid series of twists and turns before broaching and slapping its tail on the surface with unrestrained joy.

Shelley looked on amazed. Lusine could not believe what she was seeing, either. The mother had brought her baby to her deliberately to receive her touch and now showed her gratitude by placing her long snout across the nose of Lusine's board and made that strange high pitched squawking sound so familiar to the viewers of TV's wildlife shows. The dolphin mother then remained in that position, silently waiting until she also received Lusine's touch with the same energy flow passing to the beautiful sea creature.

She responded as her calf had done with an energetic brief display of chattering and splashing and then mother and calf were gone so suddenly and completely, it was as if the amazing event had not occurred.

The whole wonderful event had taken less than five minutes, but would be imprinted on the girls' memories for many years.

After the exchange of the usual OMGs and high fives, the twosome settled down as the first of the expected ocean swells began to make their presence felt. Instantly they were swivelling their heads out to sea, anticipating the waves they would ride into the shore break.

Lusine was expecting to be a little bit rusty and Shelley, who had the advantage of consistent practice, was the first to take off on a right-hander powering down the face and kicking back up into the crest repeating the manoeuvre several times before dropping off the back of the swell just as it turned into an unrideable shore break.

She turned her board and began paddling back out when she saw her friend take off on a perfect glassy wall of translucent liquid energy. What she saw was hard to believe. Lusine swept down the face, executing a strong cutback, arcing up the face once more and laying on a terrific off the lip turn. She accelerated down the wall of water and attempted a carve, but the wave got the upper hand, dumping her off the lightweight board into the foam that pounded down on her head, driving her under. All the same, it was an impressive first wave from someone who was supposed to be a bit rusty.

The morning progressed with the two girls surfing like emerging professionals until simultaneously a contrary sea breeze blew in and the tide began to ebb. The waves became increasingly unrideable with resulting chop and the two great friends retired exhausted to the beach where they towelled off and with tummies rumbling, headed for Carter's Bakery to refuel. Little Sharkbait was there as usual, trotting excitedly along beside them, anticipating his handouts from Mrs Carter.

Shelley was in awe of her friend, whose surfing skills had reached heights that were beyond her last summer and despite some winter surfing during school holidays, she had hardly had time to master some of the skills she pulled off today.

And then there was the visit from the dolphins, which was simply amazing. What was happening here?

As they sat in Carter's Bakery eating their food and sipping on cold drinks, Shelley reflected back to her salvation in the park and the very strange happening that led to her release from the deadly cancerous assault on her health. Since then, she had watched her friend Lusine taking on life's challenges with unwavering confidence creaming her exams and achieving top five percent scores state wide, absolutely crushing the requirements for her science course.

Lusine picked up her friend's thoughts as if reading her mind and told her she had something to share with her, but first she would need to be away for a day or two and if they could meet up again, she would explain a few things to her.

So the friends parted again after a brief but spectacular reunion on the water, leaving a strange air of expectancy or trepidation in the air between them.

Shelley, on the one hand, believing Lusine was holding some deep, perhaps even dark, secret from her and Lusine, trying to think of a way to explain to Shelley the extraordinary teachings she now had at her fingertips.

It was a very powerful force she could call on and she was well indoctrinated in the restraint required to administer it. Grandma Rose had reminded her frequently of the adage that power corrupts and this was not political power that the adage referred to. It was something more far-reaching. She would need to be very cautious about what she revealed to Shelley, but she knew she owed her friend some explanation. And while she trusted her very intelligent friend implicitly, she feared too much information could ruin a friendship she valued very highly. She needed time to meditate and find the right words.

Lusine had taken herself away to an isolated and very beautiful spot she knew along the coast and like some mystic guru on a mythical mountain, spent many hours in meditation clearing her mind to focus on what really was at the heart of her new world, the world of the Magus.

She was setting her course on her life's compass, deciding her direction as she went into the future. Most young people go through a similar process, generally referred to as maturing. In Lusine's case, she was now a person possessing great responsibilities due to the powers she had been granted, the weight of which was heavy on her shoulders. Given the medical studies she was undertaking, if she were to combine the two streams of knowledge, she would be a great asset to her or any community across the world.

Her thoughts were focussed on where her gifts would best be served and after deep meditation, Lusine had made her decision. It would involve a tremendous change of lifestyle, but having made the decision she felt liberated and energised.

A Sacred Dedication

Eventually Lusine had come to a point where she believed she had prepared herself well enough to reveal her story to Shelley and after breaking off her self-imposed isolation, she called her friend and arranged to meet at their favourite place, a little wind protected alcove in the headland that encircled their surf beach.

They took their boards of course, as they would have an eye out for a good swell, which was not to be ignored and as Lusine planned, they had a picnic lunch for sustenance so they could spend an unbroken day together while she delivered her story.

She found Shelley a little distracted, as in Lusine's absence, she had become acquainted with a very special boy she had been flirting with for some time and was so excited learning he was attracted to her in return, that it bubbled out of her in an excited almost nonstop babble that had Lusine rethinking her current strategy. After she had exhausted her boy talk, Shelley recognised the solemnity written all over Lusine's face and apologised, giving her friend the opportunity to say what she had come to hear.

Lusine spent several hours relating very carefully to her dear friend as succinctly as possible the story of her family inheritance. She carefully avoided any references to sorcery or magus, not wishing to appear a little eccentric.

She also avoided any mention of her status in the Armenian community as a Magus.

She explained her role as a natural healer who had powers similar to a medium in some ways, a gift that animals seemed to sense and react to like the dolphins. Although Lusine had to admit that was a huge surprise and one she will never forget.

Lusine knew now, from the tutoring received as a novice to her grandmother, that the power they had was an energy flow drawn from the natural environment. It was a source that obeyed the law of the conservation of energy, as explained in physics. The first law of thermodynamics stated energy can neither be created nor destroyed, merely changing from one form to another.

So, when the Magus draws energy from one source to transfer it to another individual in order to heal them or alter their state, the stress might deplete the strength of the Magus to resist personal illness, exposing them to mortal risk.

This thinking had become clear to Lusine in her studies. To administer to Shelley's condition, Grandma Rose had expended an enormous amount of her personal energy almost depleting her energy stocks and leaving her vulnerable. She was now in a state of physical decline, possibly due to illnesses she would have previously shrugged off.

Now Shelley was pressing Lusine for an explanation of the strange event in the park and why it had occurred so soon after their visit to her Grandma Rose, who had spoken so intensely to Shelley about her illness.

Try as she might, she could not recall a single word the old lady had said, only that it gave her great comfort and a belief that everything would be right in the long run.

Lusine would not reveal the cost to her grandmother of that personal reading, as it might be too upsetting to Shelley.

She advised Shelley that nothing would be gained by trying to recall those words, instead she should appreciate the result and be aware that Grandma Rose had been instrumental in her healing and she should be silently grateful. She apologised if saying that sounded like an admonishment, but the recipient of such a gift should never doubt it, just accept it and look for an opportunity to pay it forward by extending a hand to others in need, where she could.

Lusine believed all of nature, the totality of the environment was all interrelated and interdependent. As an example, she cited the value placed on trees, not only by environmentalists but many ancient religions and cultures, as a sacred analogy to life itself.

Environmentalists believed destroying a tree would rob the earth of a small processing plant that fed on carbon dioxide and produced the oxygen we needed to enjoy fresh air. A tree also absorbs ozone, which is a potent greenhouse gas and the shade from a single tree can save the amount of energy required to run several air conditioners.

The tree was a sacred symbol in many ancient civilisations and their religious beliefs, especially so in the history and culture from which Lusine had originated.

Shelley sat absorbed with fascination and intense concentration to Lusine's revelation and was overawed by her friend's sophistication and maturity, that appeared to have developed in very recent months. But it was undeniably impressive and she couldn't help thinking she was privileged to be in her presence and it would not be too big a stretch to imagine she was listening to one of the great thinkers of society. Well, maybe that was taking it a bit too far, but she certainly had something and that was how Shelley felt as she listened attentively to her friend's philosophies.

As the summer weeks rolled out, sometimes the surf was stunning, other times it would be a disgusting chop that only the grommets used. During one flat calm period, Shelley suggested it would be fun and interesting for Lusine to ship aboard her father's boat as he recovered his crayfish pots. Lusine was delighted with the idea, never having been out to sea like that before.

Early the next morning, in total darkness, they walked silently along the jetty to Danny McKittrick's boat, proudly named Edith for his wife and partner. Around them the dockside stirred as various other boats, targeting different species, prepared for the day ahead on the open sea or out on the blue, as Shelley romantically called it.

Shelley pointed out the different gear on the fishing boats that indicated the target species the boat's owner went after. Several boats had large drums or rollers standing vertically with fine nets wound on them. They would be fishing for snapper or similar fish. Another boat had the big rollers containing lines with hundreds of hooks. He was a 'long liner' chasing school shark. A third boat was stained heavily with squid ink on every inch of its gear and decks. No need to guess what they sought.

Shelley's dad fussed about clearing bits and pieces from the dock to the deck of his boat and when he was satisfied, he called the girls aboard handing them life jackets and without further ado fired up the huge twin diesel engines that roared into life belching blue clouds of smoke from her twin stacks and shaking the decks. Shelley jumped to, releasing the mooring lines like a seasoned crew member as she pulled the fenders inboard that protected the boat's hull from scraping against the jetty.

Danny joked that to go to sea with the fenders hanging over the side made them look like a 'Shanghai bum boat'. Whatever that was?

After what seemed a long and bouncy trip with Danny consulting his GPS, Lusine heard him throttle down and saw Shelley throw a line with a grappling hook on the end that quickly snagged the line on the first crayfish pot, identified by its distinctive marker buoy that bore his trademark DMC.

She expertly threaded the line over the spinning wheel of a winch that hauled the heavy pot up onto the deck with its catch.

The pot came on board absolutely bursting with beautiful, lively crayfish. Danny couldn't help shouting with glee at the unexpected bounty saying, it was the best first pot he had ever had. As they worked down the line of pots, each one bore its abundance from the bottom of the sea, that was soon filling the hold in unprecedented numbers.

Shelley and Danny were ecstatic, jumping about, sharing high fives with each pot more bountiful than the one before. Each crayfish was carefully measured along its shell with the smaller specimens going back into the sea before the legal sized crustaceans joined the rest of the catch in the wet hold. This specialist design allowed the sea water to freely enter the large space below the deck, keeping the catch alive for days until the boat reached port or in some cases, until prices rose.

It didn't seem long with all the excitement eating up the hours before they were heading back to port.

Shelley was telling Lusine that her father thought Lusine was a good luck charm and he could be right given the secret the girls shared between them. Danny had a smile on his face that reflected the value of the catch which, if prices were right, would pay a lot of bills and make sure they had a bit extra in the bank.

Lusine was pleased that she hadn't let herself down by avoiding seasickness.

The weather came and went in hot spells relieved by spectacular summer thunder storms which Lusine loved. The house would shake and rattle with each ear-splitting crash, following the magnificent flash of lightning. The heavy rain hammering down on the corrugated iron roof of the family's holiday home was strangely reassuring. When the storm front swept out to sea, the air was cleansed, the beach revived and everything seemed fresh and clean.

The surf was worthy of the girls' skills often enough to give them some satisfaction, but the dolphin incident was not repeated, although there was one occasion when a huge bull fur seal popped up beside Lusine's board, almost as if to greet her. He was massive and blessed Lusine with his revolting fishy breath before belching out his message with a series of coughing, dog-like barks.

He swam around and around her until he overcame his shyness and approached her within touching distance. Lusine reached over and laid her hand on his huge broad back with the same result seen with the dolphin calf, rolling over on his back, slapping his fins together and barking repeatedly before diving under the waves and disappearing out to sea. This was every bit as exciting and memorable as the dolphins and the last of these amazing events. Shelley began calling Lusine, Doctor Dolittle from the movie 'Talk to The Animals' and teased her about talking the birds down out of the trees. Lusine took it with good humour, as she knew Shelley would never embarrass her in front of others.

The summer came to a sudden end when they received a call from the family doctor informing them Grandma Rose had been admitted to hospital and was seriously ill. The family were shattered by the news and made a very quick departure back to the city.

A Dark Cloud

The news struck Lusine like a hammer blow. She had been good to her word and spoken to her adored grandmother every other day and noticed the phone calls were becoming shorter each time they spoke, as the old lady seemed to run out of breath. At no time did she complain and was more interested in Lusine's health and activities than her own situation.

Lusine said her farewell to the McKittricks who offered their best wishes. Shelley gave her a big hug and insisted Lusine keep her informed. The trip back home was interminably long and the city traffic was heavy and delayed them further. Eventually they arrived at Grandma Rose's hospital, the huge edifice dwarfing them as they entered. It was of course, one of the best hospitals in the country if not the world and their matriarch would be receiving the very best care.

Their enquiries led them to her private room somewhere in the maze of wards, teeming with very busy medical staff, all of whom seemed to be in a great hurry, mixing with slow-moving patients towing their infusion drip stands and wheelchairs, anxious visitors, cleaning staff and paramedics. It was like a human version of the traffic jams they had just negotiated. The PA system was a constant buzz of calls for Doctor So and So or Nurse Whatsit to come to...

Eventually, they found Grandma Rose's ward which thankfully, was a lot quieter where a stern but kindly matron in charge directed them to her suite.

Gabriel and Susanna questioned the matron about the old lady's condition and were told Rose was in decline as her vital organs had begun to shut down. She had not been eating and was taking sustenance intravenously.

Her worried family now made their way into her room, quietly wearing brave encouraging smiles that they failed to feel inside. They found Rose in her bed looking tiny and frail with her head and arms above the covers and her eyes closed, but as soon as she sensed their presence, she opened them and her face lit up with her customary wonderful smile. This time however, her usually brilliant blue eyes were clouded and unmistakably dim.

Susanna went to her mother and gripped her hand firmly, muttering her love and hope for her improvement. Lusine approached her from the opposite side, kissing her gently on her forehead, which felt dry and cool. The pale skin of her face looked paper thin and drawn. She could not believe how tiny and frail her grandmother looked, as if she was shrinking into the bedding. Her father stood awkwardly at the head of the bed while Susanna sat on the only available chair and held her mother's hand and they spoke quietly for some time. Then surprisingly, or perhaps not so, Grandma Rose asked to speak to Lusine privately for a few minutes. Susanna and Gabriel exchanged a knowing glance and observed her wish.

Lusine took her mother's place on the bedside chair and sat forward as Grandma Rose spoke in a voice as soft as the flutter of a butterfly's wing, causing Lusine to concentrate hard to catch every word.

She was giving Lusine what amounted to final instructions, as she assumed the role of Magus. Grandma Rose was aware of the enormity of the responsibility she was giving to her still teenage granddaughter, which was in essence a little earlier than she would have preferred. Without saying so, it was now clear this sudden weakening of her health was directly connected with the equally sudden improvement in the health of Lusine's best friend. In a roundabout way, she implied it was nothing that Lusine, or Shelley for that matter, should feel guilty about, as she had for some time prior felt her powers waning as they transferred to Lusine little by little.

Grandma Rose must have thought this would be the right time for Lusine to begin to assume her responsibilities and slowly, withdrawing her hands from her granddaughter's soft embrace, she reached up inside her neckline, taking out a gleaming golden chain that she passed over her head. On the end of the chain was a curious key, shaped like an Armenian cross with the symbol for eternity at its centre. It's weight proved it to be gold and there was no doubt it was very old. Despite this, it showed very little signs of wear.

Placing the item with great solemnity around her granddaughter's slender neck, she explained that the key allowed the holder access to the great manuscript. Without it, access was impossible. Grandma Rose warned Lusine to take exceptional care of the item for obvious reasons. From this day forward, Lusine was to be the next magus.

Grandma Rose knew full well that Lusine's love for her friend Shelley would have been a terrible temptation to use *The Blessing* to save her from her illness. She knew this would place the burden of responsibility upon her granddaughter and had sought to enact her gift and accept that consequence on herself, while she still had the power to do so. It was one very worthy cause she could influence while still able. Protect Lusine and assist her friend in her time of dire need.

'No greater love than to lay down your life for a friend.' thought Lusine and no greater example of her grandmother's generosity of spirit.

Having explained that as a final gift and the greatest gift she could impart to her, she then went on to impart some instructions to Lusine about some precious relics safely hidden in her home. Lusine would now be the keeper or curator of these sacred items, which must be protected even at the risk of losing her own life in the process. She made it sound very serious, which Lusine took to be a blood oath in importance. She was carefully instructed to go to Grandma Rose's home and from the mysterious cabinet on the second-floor landing that had held Lusine's fascination for some time, she would find these items. The beautiful sacred key Grandma Rose had presented to her would allow her entry to the cabinet. The cabinet would not open and divulge its secrets without the key.

The relics Lusine would find were a collection of rare and valuable religious icons collected by their ancestors over the centuries. An icon is a religious work of art, most often a painting. They may be carved in stone or cast in metal, painted on wood, embroidered or in the form of mosaics and usually display images of Christ, Mary or the Apostles and Angels. Lusine must make herself familiar with the contents where she would find the writings of Kusan and other mystics that will provide further evidence of the potency of the icons. Grandma Rose repeated the warning that she must not divulge any of her newly acquired knowledge or allow anyone, absolutely no one, to view the very precious items.

When Lusine's curiosity caused her to enquire about the reason for such secrecy and security, her grandmother reminded her of what she had told her earlier. That aside from the intrinsic value of the items, they would give her power others would lust after and to remember power tends to corrupt but this form of power would, in the wrong hands, corrupt absolutely. She must guard against the sacred items falling into the wrong hands at all costs.

Now the old lady suddenly appeared exhausted by the effort of speaking for so long and collapsed back even deeper into her pillows. Lusine was in tears as she was sure this was the last time she would see this precious old lady alive. Her constant mentor and confidante who had guided her through the ups and downs of her early life bestowing a legacy of self-confidence, duty, discipline and a belief in her responsibilities to her parents to be all that they expected of her. To be a kind and caring person making the absolute most of a range of skills and unique qualities she would put to work to improve the world around her. Before she called her parents in, she leaned over and fluffed up her grandmother's pillows, making her as comfortable as she could. Then she placed a soft kiss on her brow.

Lusine called her parents into the room again and they entered quietly, also knowing Rose had arrived at the last moments of her life. Susanna sat and quietly held her mother's hand and gently stroked her brow, telling her repeatedly how much she was loved. The old lady's fragile body appeared to relax and she emitted an ever so soft sigh and was gone. Lusine felt a familiar disturbance in the air as some unseen force swirled briefly around the suddenly cold sterile room, causing a slight fluttering of the window curtain, undetected by Gabriel and Susanna but Lusine had no doubt that what she had just witnessed was her grandmothers spirit leaving her body to go onto the next level of existence.

Evil Comes Calling

It is said that a vulture's eyes are powerful enough to detect an opportunity in the death of another creature from great heights and distances. It could be said the same vision was also possessed by another carrion seeker, the common real estate agent or property developer.

Lusine and her parents were besieged by all sorts of sneaky people seeking to take advantage of their bereavement, to access the beautiful home that was now Lusine's inheritance. Lusine had no trouble in seeing most of them off. On one occasion, she had come to the house to take care of a few things and found one character wearing a condescending smile below a pencil-thin moustache and holding a tape measure, a notebook and briefcase. He thrust out his hand that appeared from the ill-fitting sleeve of his cheap suit, offering his business card.

Lusine was furious and forgot her grandmother's advice about power corrupting and as the dodgy character bounded down the front steps of the property that had become her birthright, he somehow managed to stumble uncontrollably into the garden bed and before he could regain his balance, he found himself on his back in the goldfish pond. Could she have subconsciously influenced his trip? She fervently hoped so. After regaining dry land, dripping slime and mud, he sheepishly proffered his muddy card which Lusine ignored while he fled embarrassed, through the gate to never return.

Despite her anger, Lusine laughed heartily at the slapstick misfortune of the conman, his shiny suit now drooping down and covered in pond muck.

Poor little Ebony was waiting for her on the top step. He had been hiding from the stranger under one of the padded chairs on the balcony. The little dog had been spending his time with Lusine between the two homes, but always came back here looking for Grandma Rose. Poor little chap, he was inconsolable and would sniff around, hopefully trying to find a trace of his old mistress.

Lusine was spending more and more time at the old house and it was apparent the transference of *The Blessing* to her had the same transformation on the house. The gardens were show standard with a marvellous display of blooms of all sorts, which popped up in glorious disarray as though putting on a show for her. Dust and cobwebs disappeared from the interior of the house and the fine timber floors shone like gold in the morning light.

The main focus of her attention was the legendary icons and other religious items in the old solid oak cabinet upstairs in the large home. These gifts were at first mysterious and unworldly, but obviously very ancient and carried with them an aura that was almost physical. Grandma Rose had said their mysteries would unfold for her the more she read the books and writings alongside Kusan's diaries.

Her chore now was to find balance with what was at her fingertips and the life she had planned for herself.

It was not going to be easy and as if to prove the point, the doorbell rang and she was confronted by a very strange woman dressed like a cross between a gypsy and a hippie.

She claimed to be a cousin from Rose's sister's branch of the family and was very persuasive and charismatic. She introduced herself as Lusine's aunt Anahit. She had a powerfully magnetic personality and Lusine fell for her charm almost immediately and unwisely invited her in for tea, forgetting the story told to her of Anahit's banishment to Europe. To her credit, it was expected of her to act as a polite young lady should, particularly one in her position.

Lusine led the way to the kitchen as Anahit oohed and aahed over the impressive home and its beautiful furnishings. They sat at the big oak kitchen table and drank the herbal tea Lusine had prepared as Anahit began talking in a nonstop breathless stream about 'how she and cousin Rose had played together as children and how Rose had made promises of an inheritance and has the will been read, could she look around the house and maybe take one or two keepsake items in memory of her dear, dear cousin Rose, and oh how fortunate Lusine was now to be in possession of such a glorious home and at such a tender age, how on earth would she manage, did she need any assistance because she, aunt Anahit would be only too happy and look at that darling embroidered throw rug, how she would love to have something like that as a remembrance'.

Blah blah, on and on. It was like a verbal torrent that Lusine thought would never stop. This strange woman obviously had a strong sense of entitlement and was not afraid to push her cause.

Lusine was almost bowled over by the oral assault on her senses. Aunt Anahit, if that's who she truly was, had never rated a positive mention with Grandma Rose, who only spoke of her once in describing her outrageous behaviour and subsequent exile.

Anahit arrogantly announced she was going to take a look around, if that was permissible, making it quite clear she didn't care one way or the other if Lusine objected and stood suddenly, moving toward the hallway determinedly.

Lusine was suddenly outraged by this woman, whom she had only met some thirty minutes before, who was now taking her for granted and trying hard to dominate her younger relative as if she were a simple-minded child.

She jumped up and intercepted Anahit as she was preparing to mount the stairs and blocked her way firmly, making it clear she wasn't welcome to tour the house at will. Harsh words were exchanged as Lusine put the woman back in her place and told her if she felt she had a claim on the property, then she would need to make it through the family's legal representatives.

Standing firmly in front of Anahit, who persisted in trying to side step around her, Lusine finally grasped her by the upper arms and yelled at her to stop.

As she did so, a very creepy thing happened so suddenly and shockingly that it caused Lusine to catch her breath. Anahit's face appeared to blur and shift like a pixelating television image in a thunderstorm. Her face seemed to slide away like a mask, revealing a hideous manifestation behind it, glaring hatred at Lusine. Beneath the hitherto over friendly exterior dwelt something evil, leaving no doubt in Lusine's mind that here was a very dangerous presence she would need all her powers to overcome.

It was over in a flash. Instantly, Anahit switched on the charm again as she became all sweetness and light saying, "There, there, no need to be upset." She told Lusine she would take her advice and call on the lawyer, as she was sure she could make everything clear and provide evidence of her claims on the estate of her dear cousin Rose.

And as suddenly and brusquely as she had arrived, Anahit spun on her heel and marched straight out the door, failing to close it behind her. Ebony saw her off with a number of short, sharp barks at her heels that ceased abruptly after receiving an intense evil look and a snap of Anahit's bony fingers.

Lusine was shaken and deeply disturbed and immediately locked up the house, returning to her parents' home to see what they knew of this woman who claimed to be her aunt. Gabriel and Susanna were shocked to see their daughter so upset by the unexpected intrusion. Yes, they did know who she was.

She was a second cousin to Rose and her sister and had been estranged from the family when she became involved in an unhealthy form of sorcery that she had planned to use, building a network of witches or as some might call it a 'coven'. Whether this was true or even possible, it was never confirmed, only that she caused so much heartache and concern the family had universally shut her out lest she bring a contagion into their midst.

Lusine was warned to be on her guard with Anahit, whose Armenian name could mean 'sea of bitterness' in Hebrew. It seemed like a pretty good summary of her character. From childhood, she had expected more from life and failed to understand *The Blessing* chose its own and the family had not deprived her of it as they had no influence on its direction. This did not stop Anahit from her belief that she was wrongly deprived of the role of Magus by a family conspiracy.

Perhaps now, with Grandma Rose out of the way, she thought the road was clear for her to move in for a takeover.

It wasn't long before Anahit made her unwelcome presence felt again. This time forcing herself into the Levy household, to the utter disgust of Gabriel and Susanna, who seemed helpless to deflect her stream of nasty insults and threats until Lusine arrived home in time to put a stop to it.

Anahit departed angrily once more, muttering threats and curses in some strange tongue, swearing they would all regret their repeated rejection of her.

Two days later at the old house, Lusine found Ebony lying on the front veranda in a very sorry state. He whimpered pathetically when he saw her and she ran to him, scooping him up in her arms and running back to her father, yelling for him to start the car and take her to the vet. The poor little chap was still whimpering in a heart-breaking way as they rushed him into the veterinary clinic and handed him to the nursing staff. After a long wait, the doctor came out looking very glum.

He knew Ebony as Grandma Rose had been bringing him in for his annual check-up for a number of years.

He said he was baffled by Ebony's condition. At first he thought he may have taken snail bait but dismissed that, as he knew they were not used in his owner's garden. But all of Ebony's symptoms indicated he had been exposed to some form of toxic substance and the blood samples they had taken would provide the answer. He added on a more cheerful note that he expected the tough little fellow to survive, but it would be better if he stayed in the clinic overnight.

The worried family reluctantly left him in the vet's care and made their way home, where they sat around in Susanna's kitchen discussing the unusual event and its possible causes. Not surprisingly, the confrontation with Anahit and the threats she made were a little too coincidental to be ignored.

The next day, the vet rang to say Ebony's blood samples were now negative and he was ready to come home after his medical emergency. In fact, he was bouncing about the surgery full of his usual zip. The cause of his malaise was a mystery, but he had responded well to the precautionary treatments that included a sedative, which allowed him to rest comfortably overnight.

Would that be the end of Anahit's suspected incursions? They were not kept waiting long for an answer.

Several days passed and Lusine stood at the ornate front gate of the old house, gazing fondly on it, recalling the many memories it held for her. It was a picture-perfect example of its kind, very eagerly sought by people who loved this type of architecture. She knew its worth but would not sell it for anything. This was where her grandmother's spirit resided and she was sure her spirit would only depart when it was sure her legacy was safe and Lusine was secure in her role as a community leader and hereditary Magus.

She felt a huge weight of responsibility pressing down on her young shoulders and almost turned away to head back to her family home, when she felt a barely perceptible shiver of electricity run through her spine, forcing her to stand upright with its gentle push. She shook her head to clear it of all negative thoughts and stepped through the gate with the now healthy Ebony trotting in his tippy toe style alongside her happily. As they approached the front door, Lusine and Ebony both sensed something out of place at exactly the same time. The little dog stopped and growled, his hackles standing up rigidly along his spine, every muscle in his little body rigid as he backed away from the door. Lusine felt an inexplicable tremor of fear as she pushed the front door open and entered the hallway that was oddly dark and gloomy. Ebony hesitated, trembling, whining and growling as he backed away from some unseen presence not yet apparent to Lusine.

The centre of the house where the hallway terminated in a vestibule at the foot of the stairs was normally cheerfully lit by reflected sunlight, now it was shrouded in gloom as though by an unnatural shadow. Before the vestibule proper, a short passageway ran at right angles across the hallway. To the left was Grandma Rose's sitting room and to the right, the big kitchen.

Immediately ahead, the stairs bracketed by those beautifully carved balustrades, rose majestically into the upper floor of the big house. As her eyes grew accustomed to the gloom, she was horrified to see three shadowy figures seated in an arc on chairs removed from the dining room drawn up to face the front door.

The chair in the centre was occupied by the intimidating aunt Anahit, who was flanked by two equally creepy-looking women, dressed in dark gowns with full length sleeves and multiple layered petticoats over heavy pointy-toed boots, highlighted with silver adornments. They each had head coverings that were somewhere between a simple headscarf and a full Muslim hijab. Over their shoulders, they each wore wraps embroidered with strange religious symbols and illustrations of saints and angels, similar in some ways to the icons residing in the security of the old oaken cupboard upstairs. The whole scenario looked like they had come out of the costume department of a cheap movie set.

As her eyes grew more accustomed to the dim light, Lusine saw their gnarlyright hands rested on top of curiously carved walking sticks standing by their sides. They were an intimidating symbol of their menace.

Their faces were possibly the ugliest sight Lusine had ever seen outside of Halloween, twisted with cruel anger and undisguised hatred, charging Lusine's system with adrenaline. It was altogether too theatrical for words and despite the overwhelming atmosphere of threat Lusine was now in protective mode, feeling her mind sharpen and her body tense involuntarily. Confident in herself with her new status, the whole staged scenario was almost slapstick and it took all her self-control to prevent her from laughing out loud. If this ridiculous display was supposed to intimidate her with their melodramatics, they were wasting their time.

Lusine suddenly realised they looked ludicrously like the three witches from Macbeth representing the Fates: Darkness, Chaos and Conflict. She thought instantly, here was a direct challenge to her and her standing as the Magus. A shiver of fear ran through her as she comprehended she was on her own and it would be up to her to repel these dreadful grasping creatures, threatening the sanctity of the ancestral home where her grandmother's spirit still resided.

There was a moment of doubt as she confronted the evil looking trio. She knew she must dredge up the strength and courage to combat them. There was no way she could turn and run, there was too much to lose. She must stand and fight.

She would need to step carefully and forcefully here, but she did have a few tricks up her sleeve which she hoped would be a match for these old harridans. How wrong she was.

The battle commenced as the awful trio simultaneously opened their mouths wide, exposing their uneven discoloured teeth, exhaling their rank breath forcefully. The air was suddenly permeated by a foul pungency that caused Lusine to wrinkle her nose in disgust and her stomach to turn.

She stepped forward, intending to throw them out the front door like the unwelcome trespassers they were, when she was stopped in her tracks by an unbelievable sight. To her utter shock, she saw the most sacred item given in to her care under a pledge to protect it with her very life. Kusan's sacred volume! It was sitting in Anahit's lap with her left hand resting upon it. How the devil did she find it? How could she have opened the cabinet that should have protected it? The evil woman looked boldly into Lusine's eyes, tapping the brass bindings on the ancient tome with the fingernail of her middle finger. The sharp metallic sound of it echoing around the darkened space. Her wordless message was quite clear. She believed she now held the upper hand, spelled out by her arrogant body language. She demanded Lusine produce the key that would access the secrets that lay within the revered book.

Lusine had no intention of surrendering the precious key and pulled the top of her sweater up over her mouth to avoid the stench of burning sulphur emanating from the three evil ones. As she looked closely at the protective armour of the brass bindings on the mythic volume, she noticed they now bore fresh deep scratches and one or two dents where a futile attempt had been made to prise it open. Somehow, Anahit had uncovered the book from its hiding place in the locked cabinet upstairs, a feat in itself. It was obvious she had been frustrated by the impregnability of the volume's protective shield. The large ornate lock preventing access would require a key and logically Lusine would have it either on her person or hidden within the house.

Lusine knew its contents were protected by more than brass bindings and a lock. It was a power no mere mortal could overwhelm with simple brute strength. It had never been truly tested until now, but Grandma Rose had warned; woe betide to anyone who would dare to force it open without the key that now hung on a gold chain around Lusine's neck. She must fight with all her strength to prevent them from getting their hands on it.

The three sorceresses simultaneously raised their walking sticks vertically in their right hands and brought them down with a great crash on the floorboards, reverberating around the vestibule and shaking the foundations of the old house.

The clamour was a shocking assault on Lusine's ears, like a gross act of blasphemy in a cathedral. The entire house shook on its foundations with the power of the assault.

Lusine reeled back in astonishment, startled by the sudden synchronised barrage of commotion that reverberated through the house, feeling her knees weakening as her head began to spin like a child on a roundabout. As the room spun around her, she heard a thunderous sound in her ears like a roaring torrent and struggle as she might, she felt herself collapsing to the floor. She fought furiously to stay erect but the three witches slammed their walking sticks down again with the same overpowering resonance which struck her like a great gust of wind, causing her to stagger and reel about. She fell to her knees breathless and was forced to put a hand down on the floor to prevent herself from falling further. Her torment was far from over, as she could still feel the reverberations of that shocking sound.

The witches began to chant some strange dirge in unison, banging their sticks in a rhythmic thump, thump, thump. One, one, two at the same time advancing towards her in a terrifying coordinated phantasm of witchery assaulting her senses, driving her down to the floor and robbing her of her strength and the will to resist. She felt her jaw tightening and her chest compressing as they drew near, their chant seeming to grow louder and more threatening, echoing off the walls of the once peaceful haven of her childhood. The witches were bent forward with concentration, their bony left hands gesturing towards her threateningly, as though directing an unseen force against her, their faces contorted with hatred and fury.

Lusine's head throbbed with a pain that threatened to split her skull wide open as she gasped at the agony of the assault. Gamely trying to stand, she received a hammer-like blow to her back from an invisible force that took the wind out of her, knocking her to the floor. She felt her grip on consciousness slipping and as she slid into the dark void, her one comfort was the precious key to Kusan's book was hidden under her clothing close against her heart. Maybe, just maybe the evil ones would not find it.

Darkness was closing in on her; the remaining light had all but left her. She had the split-second impression of looking down a very thin dark tube to a distant spot of white light.

As the spot decreased to a micro dot, she heard something behind and under the roaring sound that had now become a howling torrent, shaking the floor she lay on. The new sound was very faint, but it persisted and grew stronger. As the sound grew in volume, it gave her a sense of ease as a comforting warmth flooded through her. There was something gently reassuring and familiar about it.

As the intensity and depth of the sound gradually built and came more clearly, Lusine recognised the unmistakeable voice of Grandma Rose. The words she spoke were unintelligible but immediately uplifting for her and instilled a much-needed jolt of strength and courage into her heart.

Aunt Anahit still held her dominant position in the centre of the dreadful trio, as they advanced on Lusine with Kusan's precious volume held shoulder high, her arm shaking with its weight or perhaps with the elation of possessing this mythical relic, still chanting the strange pulsing incantation.

Grandma Rose was the most recent but most potent Magus for many generations. She may well have passed away, but her spirit was still present in the home she had occupied for decades, reinforcing Lusine's will, recharging it like a powerful dynamo pumping energy and faith into her very core.

As she regained her strength, she began to radiate a resistance to the nightmare trio like an invisible force field. She felt herself rising from the black abyss faster and faster, an express elevator racing towards the sunlight from the bottom of a mine.

The voice of Grandma Rose had a contrary effect on the dangerous trio. The three-pronged attack began to waver and falter. First, the one on the left staggered and fell out of formation, groaning and moaning painfully, spinning about, trying to evade the contra force as though under attack from a swarm of wasps. The one on the right forged on, still stamping and chanting when her voice suddenly cracked and she uttered a hacking choking sound as if she had something stuck in her gullet. Her left hand flew to her throat, trying to ease the pressure she felt. Coughing and gagging, she staggered and went down on one knee, her eyes bulging, her already unpleasant face turning blue.

Grandma Rose's voice rose louder and more forceful booming throughout the house. Her words were uttered in an ancient language Lusine had never heard or understood, but which clearly had a profound effect on her aunt Anahit, who was now reacting like a prize fighter backing up under a welter of well-directed punches.

She still managed to hold Kusan's book above her head like the battle ensign of an advancing army, but her arm was weakening now and shaking with the strain when a brilliant golden light exploded from the sacred tome like a camera flash filling every nook and cranny of the vestibule abolishing every trace of shadow.

Anahit turned her head to look up at the book still held up in her left arm and uttered a loud scream as the impenetrable brass binding against which she had raged, began to glow with an inner heat reddening the metal until it scorched her fingers with an audible hiss.

She hung onto it determinedly, but the intense heat became too much and she was forced to drop it to the floor, where it struck with a loud thump.

Lusine regained her feet and lurched forward awkwardly, attempting to recover Kusan's miracle gift while Anahit was staggering back towards the seat she had occupied only moments before, screaming in pain and clutching her arm above the wrist, her hand a mass of nasty looking blisters. Her supporters remained where they had slumped in two untidy heaps, moaning in fear and pain and would take no further part in the fray.

There would be no respite for them or mercy shown as Ebony seized the opportunity to pounce on them, yapping furiously and snapping at any bony limbs that presented themselves. This was further incentive for the weakened pair of hags to flee the field of battle with their skirts shredded from the repeated attacks of the game little dog.

Lusine reached down to secure the sacred volume that had now cooled as it sat on the floorboards with a shadow of scorched timber outlining it. She brushed it with the back of her hand to test it for heat before picking it up, but as she stooped to do so, it simply disintegrated leaving the brass bindings collapsing into the dull grey ashes that were all that remained of the once sacred tome.

A sudden draught swirled the ashes into a solid vortex and then streamed it across the floor in a long ribbon, which shot up vertically, disappearing into the upper timbers of the stately vestibule. All that remained behind was the charred outline of the fabled volume and its now empty brass bindings where it had fallen to the parquetry floor.

A sudden profound silence fell on the mansion; the only detectable sound was the rustling of the elaborate robes of the now cowed and intimidated witches as they gathered up their remaining dignity such as it was. Whimpering and shuffling toward the front door, leaning heavily on their canes for support as Ebony continued his harassment to see the old crones off.

Anahit staggered toward the door, nursing her badly injured hand wrapped in the loose folds of her robe. She brushed by Lusine violently and deliberately, scowling and muttering curses under her breath. Her foul threats were drowned out by a thunderous voice that seemed to come from within the house itself, roaring its repulsion at the ugly intrusion on its purity.

The strange compelling voice reacted on the evil women like the angelic clarion from the bible, crushing the remaining resolve of the fleeing witches as they scrambled for the front door, pushing each other aside in their haste to depart.

As the sorceress Anahit stepped hastily through the door, she was temporarily blinded by the glaring sunlight and failed to see brave little Ebony who shot out from under the chair that had been his recent sanctuary and fastened his sharp little teeth on her ankle, giving her further cause to scream in shock and pain. She cursed and swung her foot at her attacker, tangling her heel in the hem of her gown, losing her balance along with what remained of her fractured dignity, to tumble head over heels down the steps to land in a thoroughly bruised and defeated heap.

Ebony was not finished with her yet and followed up with a series of attacks wherever he could find purchase for those deadly little fangs until Anahit, unable to fend him off, was forced to lift her skirts and flee, slamming the gate behind her.

Inside the great house, Lusine had collapsed exhausted to the floor and lay there sobbing loudly, overcome with exhaustion, grief and guilt for her inability to defend herself and the sacred book she had sworn to protect with her life. Her sobs echoed around the scene of the incredible battle and a small pool of tears formed on the polished floor beneath the crook of her arm.

How long she lay there like that, she could not say. Perhaps she fell asleep, absolutely drained by the awesome mental and physical stress of the dreadful confrontation.

She suddenly became aware of a cold wet nose nuzzling her ear as Ebony, concerned for her, returned from his sentry duty at the front gate and attempted to revive his young mistress the only way he knew how.

Sadly, she lifted her head, wiping away the tears with the hem of her skirt and still sitting on the floor, wrapped her arms around the loyal little pup, ruffling his ears and congratulating him on his bravery. His stumpy tail wagged furiously and his tiny pink tongue caught a tear that dripped down her nose. Very slowly, she became aware of an otherworldly presence in the room. Lusine felt a sudden warmth embracing her, as though an unseasonal summer breeze had blown through the door. She felt uplifted as a great weight shifted from her shoulders. Her mood transformed from despair to an exhilarating feeling of jubilation. Looking up, she was startled by a vision.

It was her much loved Grandma Rose, her familiar glowing smile on her soft gentle face surrounded by an aura of startling golden light that pulsed gently like a heartbeat.

Her image was like the many icons of angels and other holy figures Lusine was now responsible for, that lay securely in the chest upstairs. Grandma Rose's hands were held out by her sides in the classical pose, palms forward and her head turned slightly to one side in a modest posture. Lusine exclaimed her joy at her grandmother's image, which seemed to shiver slightly then straighten up, nodding her grey head towards her granddaughter in acknowledgement. Her right hand was lifted in a farewell gesture and then she was gone.

The vestibule was suddenly and deafeningly silent and empty, flooded with the natural light through the windows and the open front door which reflected from glass and polished timber.

Had this been real? It was certainly surreal! Was she still asleep and dreaming? If she was hallucinating, it was still an uplifting experience that delivered a surge of energy and self-assurance. Her weariness fell away and strength flowed into her limbs such that she felt she could almost fly. But this was only a fleeting feeling that came as the adrenaline left her system, replaced by a great weariness that flowed over her again.

Grandma's wonderful bed was waiting to provide the comfort and security she now desperately needed to hasten the healing process and reinforce the strength she had gained by overcoming this grave threat.

A Balancing Act

The showdown with the evil intentioned trio had been an exhaustive, bizarre incident mentally, physically and spiritually. Lusine dragged herself sluggishly into the kitchen and prepared some of her grandmother's amazingly restorative herbal tea that seeped into her system, revitalising her with its wonderful infusions.

After several cups, she headed for Grandma Rose's big comfy bed and collapsed across the ornate eiderdown under which she had nestled as an infant. Grandma's little warrior dog Ebony jumped up beside her and gently nestled into her side, also exhausted by his combat. Lusine's left hand dropped across his tiny sturdy body and she heard him sigh contentedly. The bedding still reassuringly carried strong traces of her grandmother's distinctive fragrances and she fell into a deep peaceful sleep that took her into a dream world where nothing had changed, where no threats or evil existed and where her Grandma Rose now resided in Glory.

When she finally awoke, it was dark and Ebony had gone, probably in search of food or water and she suddenly felt guilty for neglecting the poor little chap who had fought so gamely at her side. As soon as he was aware she was stirring, he danced into the bedroom, bouncing on his hind legs and waving his front paws excitedly, dashing back and forth trying to hurry her up as she went straight to the pantry and found his favourite foods.

Ebony attacked the bowl full of his special canned meat and a plate of crunchy treats with the same gusto as he had gone at the evil ones' ankles and cleared his plates in seconds.

Lusine became aware she herself had not eaten since her breakfast this morning at the start of a long and trying day. The kitchen clock provided a shock; it was now early morning the day after her horrible disturbance and more than twenty-four hours since she had eaten!

Her stomach growled so loudly Ebony lifted his head from his bowl, startled by the noise, perhaps fearing another attack was imminent.

The pantry and fridge were still well stocked and she fixed herself a large healthy breakfast of eggs, muesli and fruit before deciding she should return to her mother's home in case her parents were concerned for her. She cleaned up her plates and put them away and did the same with Ebony's bowl, making sure her tiny comrade-in-arms had a good drink first and then they set off after securely locking the house. Although she thought cynically, it had been secured against intrusion before!

Lusine took the usual route home, with Ebony trotting proudly alongside her as the gallant twosome entered the laneway, each with their own thoughts. Lusine's mind churned with the recollection of the horrible confrontation on the previous day when faced with a deadly evil that threatened her very life.

The destruction of Kusan's book, the very soul of *The Blessing*, entrusted to her by her grandmother for safe keeping for future generations was the main heart-breaking loss.

Ebony on the other hand, may well have been thinking of the pleasure of sinking his needle-sharp teeth into the bony ankle of the creature who threatened his mistress. Ebony had long since become accustomed to thinking of the girl as his new mistress. Many animals and in particular dogs, have a sense of mortality and Ebony was aware his previous mistress had departed and that his duty now lay with the girl alongside him.

Lost in their independent thoughts, the triumphant survivors of the perilous combat entered the park with their defences down. What they encountered was a shocking sight.

The entire grass surface of the park was covered by a dense inky black gathering of noisy squabbling ravens, squawking loudly, flapping and pecking at each other.

A gathering of ravens may be called a 'conspiracy' or even 'unkindness' of ravens. These are highly appropriate terms for the evil looking birds that were now carpeting Lusine's beloved park.

What was the meaning of this distressing sight? Was this more of the work from the wicked trio? Could she expect things like this to continue in the days ahead?

Her anger and frustration burst from her in a shrill scream as she threw her hands up to the sky in rage.

The ravens reacted to her dramatic gesture like a symphony orchestra to its conductor, erupting into the air in a raucous screeching churning mass that resembled the black ashes from a paper fire rising directionless on the hot air, swirling, diving and arcing across the sky.

Lusine was astounded by the amazing display as the large conspiracy of ravens gathered height and swept up over the tree tops in a ragged noisy stream that swirled high around the park before disappearing rapidly from sight and sound leaving the park to return to its normal state. If this intriguing patch could ever be described as normal.

With the sudden resumption to tranquillity, Lusine was struck by the thought that the ravens had responded to her unspoken revulsion and her wish they would simply disappear. Had her new found status and its powers influenced them, she might never know?

As if to reinforce that thought she felt a familiar rush of air as her old friend the invisible force swept over her, heading for the far corner of the park and she now knew her grandmother, now succumbed, had not really left her and would be there guiding her and supporting her until such time as she fully assumed her responsibilities as a mature Magus.

The loss of Kusan's book may not be the total disaster she initially thought it would be.

Perhaps now, reduced to ash, its powers still resided in the framework of Grandma Rose's wonderful home where it would now forever dwell. As for the home itself, she would remain its owner, curator and protector for as long as she lived. As these thoughts crowded her mind, she felt a familiar warm, uplifting sensation pass through her body again while a great weight of uncertainty seemed to lift from her shoulders. Her mind felt remarkably clear of concern for her own future and the responsibilities she would need to shoulder.

She may have stood there contemplating these facts for some time and may have continued to do so if Ebony had not scratched at her leg and whimpered. Snapping out of it, she reached down and scratched his ears as she resumed her walk.

Ebony recovered quickly from the stunning sight of the mass of ravens that had set him back on his haunches a little, but now as the girl moved confidently across the park, heading in a familiar direction, he was reassured and took up his station beside her right leg.

There were no further acts of sorcery on the remainder of the short trip home and Lusine pushed through her father's front gate and entered the family home with a cheerful hello.

Her parents, who had feared further confrontation with Anahit, both bustled out of the kitchen and rushed towards her with their arms outstretched and their faces etched with concern.

When they saw the big smile on Lusine's face and heard the happy yapping of her little four-legged soldier, they knew instinctively she was just fine.

Thereafter, the year rolled out as it should, with no further interruptions as Lusine completed her first year of a Bachelor of Medical Science at Melbourne University.

A high-achieving student such as Lusine could apply to complete a research project in an area of special interest. Her ultimate desire was to work in paediatrics, helping to find a way to make the lives of ill children more positive in one of the major hospitals and her progress so far almost guaranteed it.

Summer Break

It would be very odd if the Levys failed to holiday at Port Isaac in the summer and this year, despite everything, was to be no different. Lusine and her family arrived and went through the familiar routine of unpacking, dusting and restocking the pantry and fridge.

As usual, she met Shelley at their beach very early on the first morning in a joyful reunion. Lusine had brought her paddle board this time, wheeling it down to the beach on a small trolley that also carried her paddle. Shelley chided her about getting old and cautious until Lusine pointed out the complete lack of swell and told her, while she sat on the beach waiting for a wave that might not come, she would at least be out on the water enjoying the ocean and getting some much-needed exercise.

Ebony had come with her to Port Isaac after her grandmother had first been admitted to hospital and had immediately bonded with Sharkbait, Shelley's little dog that was still a keen surfer and so far, thank heavens yet to fulfil the fate of his name.

Lusine wasn't going to waste the glorious day ahead and without a backward glance to her friend, launched her board with Ebony jumping aboard, as she paddled out into the deeper blue. The early morning sun was yet to claim sole ownership of the heavens above, but was still sweeping the stars away to the west.

Away on the far eastern horizon, a few tufts of cotton-wool clouds had their bottoms shaded a light pink by the rising sun.

They were low on the distant horizon, moving imperceptibly with glacial slowness at the behest of a slight sea breeze and could signal a summer thunderstorm later in the day.

But for the moment, they were too far distant to be a concern. Lusine paddled out, the only sound being the dip and swirl as the sea water ran off the blade of her paddle.

Soon she found herself well out to sea beyond where she or Shelley would normally go in pursuit of an ocean swell. The sea-swell stirred her with a very gentle, barely discernible uplifting of her board. The glassy surface reflected the remaining brighter stars above, contesting the rising sun. The sea was a deeper, darker blue with the bottom forty feet below only visible as patches of browns and very dark greens as she drifted over rocky reefs. The resident groves of kelp were home to many species of fish in rich variety, visible as silvery flashes as they hunted or evaded predators. It was quite beautiful.

Ebony sat on the nose of the board with his little pink tongue hanging out gazing about, lost in his own thoughts while his mistress sat cross legged in the middle, meditating and chanting quiet incantations of peace and love she had recently learned, when she abruptly became aware Shelley had paddled up quietly beside her, snapping her out of her meditative mood. Shelley was tracking the distant cloud formations, wondering out loud if Lusine thought there was a storm on the way. Lately, Lusine had become a pretty accurate weather forecaster, among her other talents. She was no longer a teenage girl finding her way in the world. She was now a self-assured young woman, well on her way to finding her purpose in life. Shelley was just about to speak again when suddenly Ebony barked sharply at a pod of dolphins that burst from the sea.

The pod was a family and Lusine was sure it was the mother and calf she had met some time ago. Now here was that friendly dolphin with her complete family unit: bull, cow and calf.

As the sun crept above the horizon, it cast a fan of beautiful rays that spread out through the low clouds, and against this background, the family of dolphins performed for the two friends. Diving deep and accelerating from below to launch their sleek glistening bodies into clear air, emitting high pitched squeaking and clicking sounds trailing a perfect arc of seawater behind them. It was a wonderful display and one few people were privileged to see in the wild.

Shelley had no doubt it was her friend's influence that brought them here and she knew she would witness many such wonders at Lusine's side in the years ahead. She believed she had received her own blessing on the day they met and she would be forever grateful to this miraculous girl and her mysterious grandmother who had sacrificed her own health so that she, Shelley would survive.

She was determined to see that Grandma Rose's sacrifice would not be in vain, by serving her memory and the community. Wherever possible, she would be at Lusine's right hand whenever she was needed.

Was it sorcery Lusine possessed, enabling her to influence circumstances in her sphere? Was she a white witch with truly paranormal powers? The one thing Shelley was sure of, her friend was truly motivated by compassion and generosity.

It is often said that truth can be stranger than fiction and miracles were a well recorded phenomenon in the history of the world.

Shelley considered the things she had seen and experienced personally with Lusine and had come to the conclusion it didn't matter whether they were magus or miraculous. Perhaps the real answer was the powerful positive energy Lusine radiated and the love she bestowed on her family and friends.

Was it possible the 'miracles' Shelley had witnessed resulted from Lusine's resolute love of humanity and the world around her? That compelling optimism she radiated was an irresistible force that could break down the walls of despair and replace it with hope. Was that the real magus? And could she, Shelley McKittrick, learn from the example of her friend and teach that attitude to others? Time would tell as the years ahead rolled out.

But in the meantime, there would be those wonderful summer days to look forward to at Port Isaac, sitting on their boards out the back waiting for that perfect six-foot glassy swell with her remarkable friend.

The End

Shawline Publishing Group Pty Ltd
www.shawlinepublishing.com.au

9 781922 850089